Rapture of the Deep

Rapture of the Deep

Reflections on the Wild in Art,
Wilderness and the Sacred

Doug Thorpe

RED HEN PRESS | *Los Angeles, California*

Rapture of the Deep:
Reflections on the Wild in Art, Wilderness and the Sacred

Copyright © 2007 by Doug Thorpe

ALL RIGHTS RESERVED

No part of this book may be used or reproduced in any manner whatsoever without the prior written permission of both the publisher and the copyright owner.

Book design: Richard O. Niño
Cover design: Mark E. Cull

ISBN: 978-1-59709-055-1
Library of Congress Catalog Card Number: 2007926597

The City of Los Angeles Department of Cultural Affairs,
Los Angeles County Arts Commission
and the National Endowment for the Arts
partially support Red Hen Press.

Published by Red Hen Press

First Edition

Acknowledgements

When people ask me how long this book has taken, I tell them that my daughter—who's eight-years-old in the first essay—is now twenty-three, out of college and on her way to graduate school.

Plenty long.

I'm grateful to those who have helped bring it forth, beginning with Laurie and Larry David for their decision to create the David Family Environmental Book Award, which most immediately made this book possible. I'd also like to thank the judges for this award: Alison Deming, Robert F. Kennedy Jr, and Carl Pope.

Thanks as well to those who kindly supplied feedback and literary support—Scott Cairns, David James Duncan, Bill McKibben, John Elder, Marc Hudson—and, more generally, to those who gave either friendship or inspiration (or both): Denise Levertov, whom I still miss, John Haines, Craig Rennebohm.

Much appreciation goes to Albert Fisher, whose own work inspires me, and, more to the point, whose painting graces the cover of this book.

Gratitude goes to the journals where a number of these essays were first published: *Parabola, Image, Mars Hill Review, Terra Nova.*

Support has also been appreciated from family and friends, including a number of communities of whom I'm fortunate to be a part: my colleagues at Seattle Pacific University, and in particular in the English department (a bow to Mark Walhout, chair); friends at the Center for Spiritual Development—above all its director, Jerry Hanna, who lead many of the meditation retreats that inform this book; and to friends at St. Mark's Cathedral, including the Dean, Robert Taylor, and the staff, and in particular to Carla Berkedal Pryne (who talked me into editing *Earth Letter* back in her days as Director of Earth Ministry), to Jim and Ruth Mulligan and my friends on the Ecology-Spirituality committee.

Above all I thank my wife, Judy Andrews, and our daughter, Katie Thorpe, without whom this book would not be. They know all that is in these pages, and all that has been left out. It is to them that I dedicate it.

This book is for my wife, Judy Andrews,
and our daughter, Katie Thorpe

Contents

Introduction	1
I Pitched at the Brink	22
Interlude: Casper David Friedrich: Wanderer above the Mists	41
II Of Rivers and Religion	46
Interlude: Crossing the Threshold	62
III Walking Among the Fires	68
Interlude: Shadows on the Land	98
IV Death Enters the Wilderness Singing	101
Interlude: The Shadow, The Twins, and the Mall of America	113
Conclusion	120

The First Words (from the *Romanian of Marin Sorescu*)

> *The first words got polluted*
> *Like river water in the morning*
> *Flowing with the dirt*
> *Of blurbs and the front pages.*
> *My only drink is meaning from the deep brain,*
> *What the birds and the grass and the stones drink.*
> *Let everything flow*
> *Up to the four elements,*
> *Up to water and earth and fire and air.*
>   —Seamus Heaney,
>   *The Spirit Level*

The man in the forest reacts to his problems by creating culture. To that end he manages to retreat from the forest and withdraw into himself. There is no creation without withdrawing into oneself. Well then, the man who is too cultivated and socialized, who is living on top of a culture which is already false, is in urgent need of another culture, that is to say a culture which is genuine. But this can only start in the sincere and naked depths of his own personal self. There he must go back to make contact with himself. But this cultivated self, the culture which he has received from without, and which is now decrepit and devoid of evidence, prevents him from doing this. . . . Thanks to culture, man has gotten away from himself. . . . So he has no other course than to rise up against that culture, to shake himself free of it, so that he may once more face the universe in the live flesh and return to living in very truth.
  —Ortega y Gasset, *Man and Crisis*
   quoted in John Haines,
   Living Off the Country

Rapture of the Deep

Introduction

In Colorado two teenage boys walk into their suburban high school with a plan, guns, and enough rage to take down the universe. They are desperadoes waiting for the noon train. They are the wild ones, riders from the apocalypse. They are the truth returning like radioactive waste. It seems that they learned nothing in school but this.

At the same time, in Kosovo what we call "the Balkan Question" is being similarly answered. As child psychiatrist, Lynne Mastnak, writes, in the town of Livovc only 15 of 170 houses remain undamaged. "The white school building and the cultural center are gutted; the small clinic is a pile of rubble; teenagers are selling cheap biscuits, chewing-gum and cigarettes on upturned milk crates." She talks to one girl who explains that shells killed her father and two sisters as he tried to load the family onto a tractor. She herself was wounded and watched her little sister die on the way to the doctor. Another child describes how he and his father, his 20-year-old brother and two uncles were taken by the police, stripped naked and badly beaten. Then, because his father pleaded for his life, the boy was allowed to escape. He wandered in the woods for two days until he found his way home.

Up in the Pacific Northwest a few members of the Makah Indians hunt a gray whale before a national television audience, leading to an explosion of verbal (and at times physical) abuse against not just the Makah but all Indians, just as if the Norwegians and the Japanese haven't been "harvesting" whales all along. One of my students tells of seeing a logging truck with a bumper sticker reading *Kill Indians Not Whales.*

Meanwhile I teach classes on the American West, on English Romanticism, and a new Freshman class on "The Call of the Wild." My daughter, who is fifteen and a freshman in high school, reads pieces of *The Odyssey* and *Gilgamesh*, meaning that as a teacher of literature I am once again in demand. As she works on essays we talk intensively of the ideas in these books—of the Greeks and rationality, the idea of the hero. And as we talk it suddenly strikes me: she's walking this same road of the Greeks even as she reads and struggles to write. These skills *are* that road. Analysis—that ability to stand apart and observe objectively—is the method we've chosen to carry us home. It's a path so familiar that we don't always realize that there might be alternative routes through this wilderness.

All of these events become like pieces of a puzzle, like tangled threads. I'm reminded of the old Grandmother in Leslie Silko's novel, *Ceremony*, who says, "it seems like I already heard these stories before . . . only thing is, the names sound different."[1] And then I remember a recent *New Yorker* cartoon, where two old men are sitting in comfortable armchairs while they talk about the war in the Balkans. One man turns to the other and says, "This is where I came in."

It is, of course, where we all came in. And I don't just mean World War I; a quick glance through *Gilgamesh* will remind us that our current situation has very deep roots. The oldest extent piece of written literature, it's the story of a man who determines to make a name for himself—to set up "a monument to the ego" in William Irwin Thompson's words—by making war on the cedar forests. Slaying the "demon" of the woods, a being sacred to the Queen of Heaven, causes the death of his best friend, and in turn leads the hero on a long and failed journey through the wilderness, always seeking to overcome his own mortality.

When I teach this book these days, over four thousand years after its words were first set down on stone tablets, students generally get it immediately. And no wonder: in spite of the Internet and word processing we recognize the terrible fear that haunts this man. *Gilgamesh wandered in the wilderness / grieving over the death of Enkidu / and weeping saying "Enkidu has died. /Must I die too? Must Gilgamesh be like that?"* It's very simple, and nothing about it has changed or dated. We're invited into the company of that first conscious human, the one "who knew the most of all men know; who made the journey. . . ."[2]

Introduction

There are, as Robert Frost might say, two roads diverging in this wood. One, the road of Gilgamesh, or what we might call the road west, takes the wood from that forest and from it makes a city as a monument to his own magnificence. He stands before his handiwork with pride—or, as an old man, with resignation. *Study the brickwork,* he says, *study the fortification; this is Uruk, the city of Gilgamesh.*

Another road, however, leads us more deeply into these woods, with a different goal in mind. As Thompson suggests, the sage who tests Gilgamesh at the end of his quest is much less interested in physical strength than in spiritual insight. "What this introvert is saying to the great extrovert is, in effect, 'You have slain lions, O great hero, but can you slay your own mind?'"[3] Told to stay awake for six nights and seven days, Gilgamesh fails within minutes.

This sage shows us the other road we might walk into the wilderness. Somewhere in that forest he has tasted not just fear but wonder. He has known the rolling waters of the sea, the great silence of the mountains, and in those places has felt something so huge and beautiful that he's ready to surrender everything to be part of it.

I want in these pages to follow the thread of this rapture. I call that thread "the wild."

Describing the landscape on the Greek Island of Lesbos, the poet Linda Gregg said to an interviewer:

> I was starved for something, and that seemed to get mixed in with a presence I felt there which I seemed always just about to glimpse. I began to call that presence which I sensed so strongly, to call that "thing" Her. I would say to myself or to people I knew, "I have to go to the big pine tree in the olive orchard today. . . . I have to go to the stone winnowing ring up on the mountain they don't use anymore. . . ." Feeling I might see something of her. It sounds artificial, I know; but it wasn't. What I felt was nothing like posturing. And it wasn't really pleasant. It was like being haunted, almost painfully. Still I kept at it. I wasn't passive. I worked hard to hunt down whatever it was there that I needed to find. And once in awhile I would almost see it.[4]

"It was like being alive twice," Gregg writes in another context. So too do we hear from Robert Hass, who writes of the rapture of images. They haunt us, he says:

> Cézanne painting 'till his eyes bled, Wordsworth wandering the Lake Country hills in an impassioned daze. Blake describes it very well, and so did the colleague of Tu Fu who said to him, "It is like being alive twice." . . . In the nineteenth century one would have said that what compelled us about them was a sense of the eternal. And it is something like that, some feeling in the arrest of the image that what perishes and what lasts forever have been brought into conjunction, and accompanying that sensation is a feeling of release from the self. Antonia Machado wrote, *"Hoy es siempre todavía."* Yet today is always. And Czeslaw Milosz, *"Tylko trwa wieczna chwila."* Only the moment is eternal.[5]

Call it the sublime, call it the Tao, Om, or I AM; still the names don't hold. As Laurens Van Der Post says, "The moment you try to control it, there is no revelation."[6] Always difficult to define, and for most of us immensely difficult to inhabit for long, what lies within these images is an unnamed place of depth and recognition. Stephen Levine experiences this as he watches a friend die in a state of pure surrender. "Open space," he calls it.[7]

The following essays attempt to move inside this space. By way of narratives that wander through mountains and rivers, through art and literature, and through the realms of mysticism and the mundane, they ask in a dozen different ways: where do we go to meet up with ourselves?

Arjuna's answer to this question comes from Krishna, Job's from a whirlwind, and Lao Tzu's from a hundred rivers flowing to the sea. Dante is ravished into response by the sight of Beatrice, Rumi by his beloved Shams. This truth is in the desert that Moses enters; for a Christian it's the desert that Jesus *is*. He carries wilderness wherever he goes; to meet him is to enter an unending expanse.

It's there in Georgia O'Keefe's landscapes and in the Ancient Mariner's wide sea. It's in the paintings of Caspar David Friedrich and Vincent Van Gogh, and in what one critic calls the "dark archaic gates" of Mark Rothko. "Nothing burns in hell but self-will," writes the

Introduction

fourteenth century author of the *Theologica Germanica*. This, too, is what wilderness is for.

One of the best living defenders of the wild, and one who comes close to defining it by *living* it, is Gary Snyder, who neatly clarifies the distinction between wilderness, wildness and the wild, suggesting that the latter may well be a synonym for the Tao—"The Way of Great Nature":

> eluding analysis, beyond categories, self-organizing, self-informing, playful, surprising, impermanent, insubstantial, independent, complete, orderly, unmediated, freely manifesting, self-authenticating, self-willed, complex, quite simple.[8]

At the heart of this paradox is a wildness that is both complete in itself, as Snyder says—that rests deeply in its own Being—and yet is also deeply present in the ongoing processes of life. It (or He or She) is both emptiness and fullness, both the void before creation and the Big Bang that begins it. This is the energy that says "Be still and know I am God" and that also drives evolution. This energy forms DNA as a stable means of reproducing life, and then introduces genetic mutation, which, as Thomas Berry and Brian Swimme write, is itself "a primal act of life."[9] DNA is inherently conservative: the very fact that many of the genes found in human beings are also found in mushrooms would suggest this principle of conservation. And yet mutation suggests that change is a radical force *within* conservation, for without change, without the ability to adapt, every living thing is doomed to extinction.

Mutation is itself *part* of life. It's not a *thing;* rather, it makes possibility possible. It's the wild card, that infinite field inside the smallest of things.

If we were to give this possibility a name, and if we were mythologically oriented, we might call it Hermes, "the adept who can move between heaven and earth, and between the living and the dead." He is, as Lewis Hyde says, a boundary-crosser. He's the creator of culture, the bringer of *techne*—from whence we get technology—and he is the force "whose function is to uncover and disrupt the very things that cultures are based on."[10] That very disruption is what brings into being another culture, another cosmos, and thus another shot at life.

He's Prometheus, Coyote, and Raven. He's Christ disguised as a thief in the night.

"Chance and accident," Hyde quotes, "are an intrinsic part of primeval chaos [and] Hermes carries over this peculiarity of primeval chaos—accident—into the Olympian order." Hermes is wildness *deified*, admitted as eternal, as part of the very order that his nature appears to disrupt.

Which again suggests that there is an order deeper than the order that resists all change, an order that knows disorder—creativity—as part of its inherent order.

"The bottom of the mind is paved with crossroads," Paul Valery writes, which is another way of saying that in order to know something of Hermes—that god of the crossroads—we must go beneath the mind's own desire for order. We must sit with ourselves in the void, which is no place at all.

Existing outside of space and time, existing before existence itself, this reality also exists *within* space and time. In each "minute particular," as Blake says, "there's a moment in time that Satan cannot *find*." It's a kind of gap, that place where God "emptied himself" so that life could exist.

> Thirty spokes converge on a hub.
> But it's emptiness
> that makes a wheel work[11]

writes Lao Tzu, meaning, I believe, that all the turning in the universe depends upon this underlying and unnamable quality—this originating force.

Consider, for a contemporary experience of this deeper wildness, the unusual journey of Richard Erdoes. Raised in Vienna, Berlin, Budapest, and Paris—centers of western civilization—he describes his first response to a western American landscape:

> We had been driving all day through corn country, flat and rather monotonous—widely spaced farms with white picket fences. . . . We crossed the Missouri and the old highway began to undulate, dip and rise, dip and rise, roller-coaster fashion. We drove over one dip and suddenly found ourselves in a different world. Except for the road, there was no sign of man. Before me stretched an endless ocean of hills, covered with sage and prairie grass in

shades of silver, subtle browns and ochers, pale yellows and oranges. Above all this stretched the most enormous sky I had ever seen. Nothing in my previous life had prepared me for this scene of utter emptiness which had come upon me without warning.

This is the wilderness experience: that big sky, the enormous emptiness. But it isn't fear that arises in Erdoes; instead, he writes, "I found myself overwhelmed by a tremendous, surging sensation of freedom, of liberation from space[.] I experienced a moment of complete happiness."

Later that night he thought again about his emotional response to this barren landscape:

> It was not beautiful in the accepted sense of the word. It was not pretty. Yet it had more of an impact upon me than the stained-glass windows of the Sainte-Chapelle, the hills of Rome, the Austrian Alps or the Loire Valley, which are all, by common consent, called "beautiful." I think it was a sense of being completely swallowed up by nature that gave the prairie its powerful attraction. . . . Even high up on a Swiss glacier one is still conscious of the toy villages below, the carefully groomed landscape of multicolored fields, the far away ringing of a church bell. It is all very beautiful, but it does not convey the prairie's sense of liberation, of losing oneself, of utmost escape.[12]

The classic "groomed landscape" of civilization is a precise image for what we seem to leave behind. As a result we are—like Jonah—"swallowed up by nature." In this wilderness of mountain and sky, as in all the deep places of the heart, we return to something simple and essential. Lost inside its great expanse we come to know our place. We learn humility, whose roots come from *humus*. This wilderness is where we learn again to be human.

Which is why it's always the way home.

In such comparisons—that "carefully groomed landscape" versus the prairie's "utter emptiness"—an old opposition between civilization and wilderness returns. And yet in spite of Erdoes I'm less interested in their opposition than I am in the continuum I see between them. "Opposition is true friendship," Blake insists, which in this context means that the wild and the cultured—like the raw and the cooked, the sublime and the beautiful—are inevitably in relationship with each other, and in relationship to something deeper than either.

"The good worker loves the board before it becomes a table," Wendell Berry writes, "loves the tree before it yields the board, loves the forest before it gives up the tree."[13] This worker isn't civilizing the savageness out of the tree; instead she loves some broader and deeper nature from which that wood derives, and which must in some way remain in the table. Her work is nothing more than another expression of that nature; the table's beauty depends on its possessing something of the sublimity of its origins.

Another version of this relationship (and another answer to *Gilgamesh*) comes from Chuang Tzu's woodworker Ch'ing, who explains how he comes to manifest the Tao—this underlying pattern which all things follow—in a beautiful bell stand:

> When I am going to make a bell stand, I never let it wear out my energy. I always fast in order to still my mind. When I have fasted for three days, I no longer have any thought of congratulations or rewards, of titles or stipends. When I have fasted for five days, I no longer have any thought of praise or blame, of skill or clumsiness. And when I have fasted for seven days, I am so still that I forget I have four limbs and a form and body. By that time, the ruler and his court no longer exist for me. My skill is concentrated and all outside distractions fade away. After that, I go into the mountain forest and examine the Heavenly nature of the trees. If I find one of superlative form, and I can see a bell stand there, I put my hand to the job of carving; if not, I let it go. This way I am simply matching up "Heaven" with "Heaven."[14]

He wishes to forget ambition, the anxiety around success and failure, and so he fasts to "still his mind." In this way he journeys far from his daily routine. In his rigorous discipline he faces whatever we meet inside this wilderness of silence: hunger, pride, fear, desire. He listens, waiting in the emptiness. He is seeking something and his way of finding it is by letting himself be found. As the footnote says, he matches up "his own innate nature with that of the tree."

"To learn to preserve the fertility of the farm," Sir Albert Howard writes, "we must study the forest." These words, like Chuang Tzu's, represent a way of knowing far different from the notion that cultiva-

Introduction

tion eliminates (or enlightens) the wilderness. Instead it hints that we cannot truly know ourselves as human until we've crossed back into this forest home out of which we came. And while we may not literally stay in that wilderness, neither do we leave it behind. What else is baptism's meaning? *You are marked as Christ's own forever.* Christ is one name we give to that forest, that infinite sky, which in turn are simply names for some experience which must go nameless. Christ's mark—a wooden cross—inscribes a way of being in the world that is without boundaries. That mark tells us who we are: it matches our own innate nature with that of the tree.

True work of any sort begins with this journey into what one theologian calls "forest dwelling," which, among many other things, is "an existential protest against the shallowness of everyday experience and everyday talk."[15] This is why Thoreau fled to the woods of Walden, avoiding life in the parlor, where, as he puns, conversation is merely parliamentary. This too is why we respond so deeply to Whitman's great call to

> Sail forth—steer for the deep waters only,
> Reckless soul, exploring, I with thee and thou with me,
> For we are bound where mariner has not yet dared to go,
> And we will risk the ship, ourselves and all.

Forest dwelling, whether at Walden Pond, at the edge of the sea, or at someone's bedside, is the soul's hunger for depth, for truth, for all things just. It's that risk of which poet, philosopher and animal trainer Vicky Hearne speaks when she says that she had "fallen in love with this horse, and while love is a dangerous guide, there are parts of the forest we sometimes find ourselves in that no other guide even guesses at the existence of." As in so many of Shakespeare's comedies, we are led into this forest by love, which in turn demands of us a new way of being in our old world.

All of these words—Whitman's and Erdoes', Chuang Tzu's and Vicki Hearne's—return us to this sublimity that runs like a river through things. They each take risks for the sake of a deeper reality which brings, as Hearne says, not "the glamour of winning . . . [but] the glamour of being fully alive."[16]

Rapture of the Deep

What we experience in these moments is not so much a description of something "out there" as an awakening to something *in here*. We look on, offering homage not to the outer form but (in Coleridge's words) to "the infinity of our own souls which no mere form can satisfy."[17] It is ourselves we meet in this place. We are invited to see *by means of* this: to *own it* in the sense of knowing that this way of being is profoundly and fundamentally who we are.

It's a very old story. When asked by disciples about his real identity, the Buddha simply says, "I am awake." So too with Jesus, who says "before Abraham was, *I am.*" Both invite us not to follow the law but to know ourselves *as* the law.

"Awareness is a wild thing," Joel Kramer writes. This gets it exactly: wildness is a way of seeing, whether this truth comes to us through the open expanse of a wilderness landscape or through the minute particulars of the dance, the poem, or a three minute rock and roll anthem. It's the Way of Great Nature.

While they live in perpetual opposition, wilderness and the beauty cultivated from it are both invitations to awareness. Our bodies themselves are temples to this truth: infinite space inside of finite form.

Genuine safety demands the genuinely heroic, Vicki Hearne writes. The frames of civilization—of marriage and garden, as of sonnet and haiku—are there, potentially, not to make the world safe from wilderness but as a way to "match [our] own innate nature with that of the tree." This is what makes a marriage *more* than human law. It returns marriage—and poetry—to the deepest roots of law, which lie in patterns of *li*, or "the order and pattern in Nature, not formulated Law." This, Joseph Needham writes, "is dynamic pattern as embodied in all living things, and in human relationships and in the highest human values."[18]

When Czeslaw Milosz wrote to Thomas Merton that he didn't understand the idea of Providence, Merton responded with characteristic directness: "Insofar as we are in Christ, we are our own Providence. The thing then is not to struggle to work out the 'laws' of a mysterious force alien to us and utterly outside us, but to come to terms with what is inmost in our own selves, the very depth of our own being."[19]

There are many ways of expressing this truth, as many ways as there are cultures. *Form is emptiness, emptiness is form* is how the *Heart Sutra*

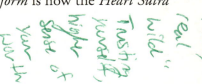

puts it; form is the wave and emptiness the sea, Thich Nhat Hanh explains.[20] He is speaking of us, of course, of Gilgamesh, myself, my daughter. He's also speaking of an entirely different sort of education, where the real hero is the one who comes to see her form as a wave of this sea, both ephemeral *in this form* and yet forever part of the waters out of which all life arises.

Form is the wave. . . . Form is what life strives for; it is, I'm tempted to say, what life loves. If a nation's motto can be *e pluribus unum*—out of the many one—life's motto might be out of the one, many. But these forms are inherently impermanent; whether of the individual or of nations the form isn't intended to last. Democracy itself, as Frances Moore Lappe suggests, "is process—the way, not the goal." It is that sea out of which each of us expresses ourselves. It is what makes us possible.

We too are noble animals, as Vicki Hearne tells us. "I mean that we are born to it, born to the demands of the heroic, of a pleasure earlier than love and nearer to heaven, the pleasure of the heroic approach to knowledge of form." This is our work, our laboring upon the world not to make our lives safe but to make them deep and full.

Civilization's long, heroic journey may well reside in a continual quest for this knowledge of form, which in turn leads us back to the rapture of the deep. Our way lies in an unwillingness to settle for anything less than beauty.

Whatever we call it, this wilderness is also who we are, however much we might wish to forget. When Robert Frost says "I have been one acquainted with the night," we know what he means, even if we can't easily explain it. So too when he writes:

> They cannot scare me with their empty spaces
> Between stars—on stars where no human race is.
> I have it in me so much nearer home
> To scare myself with my own desert places.

Frost—like others before and after—writes from a perspective that sees this emptiness as pure negation. But it may instead be that forest dwelling is where we move out of the parlor and into the deep places of the heart. Here we are left without a map, and even without a road.

And yet we know somehow that this wilderness—this truth—is exactly what we need, however much we avoid it. Our souls drink it. This place is the milk of the holy.

Failing to embrace the shadows within, attempting too often to civilize our darkness away, we continually miss the meeting with the Beloved. After all, the fierce "Dark Night of the Soul" that John of the Cross describes is in truth a lover's tryst.

> By dark of blessed night,
> In secrecy, for no one saw me
> And I regarded nothing
> My only light and guide
> The one that in my heart was burning.

Speaking of the Desert Fathers, those early hermits of the Christian church who fled the cities to live in solitude in the deserts of the Middle East, Thomas Merton writes,

> What the Fathers sought most of all was their own true self, in Christ. And in order to do this, they had to reject completely the false, formal self, fabricated under social compulsion in "the world." They sought a way to God that was uncharted and freely chosen, not inherited from others who had mapped it out beforehand . . . Obviously such a path could only be traveled by one who was very alert and sensitive to the landmarks of a trackless wilderness. The hermit had to be a man mature in faith, humble and detached from himself to a degree that is altogether terrible. The spiritual cataclysms that sometimes overtook some of the presumptuous visionaries of the desert are there to show the dangers of the lonely life—like bones whitening in the sand.[21]

What they sought in the desert was *quies,* rest. But this rest, Merton says, "was a kind of simple no-whereness and no-mindedness that had lost all preoccupation with a false or limited 'self.' At peace in the possession of a sublime 'Nothing' the spirit laid hold, in secret, upon the 'All'—without trying to know what it possessed."

To most of our ears, of course, such a life sounds extraordinary. And yet the paradox remains: what they sought was precisely the ordinary.

Introduction

"The simple men who lived their lives out to a good old age among the rocks and sands only did so because they had come into the desert to be themselves, their ordinary selves, and to forget a world that divided them from themselves."

The ordinary: this is close, I think, to what Linda Gregg sought in the brown hills of Greece, what Thoreau sought at Walden—and, for all of the outer differences, it's what Nora Helmer sought beyond that slammed door at the end of *A Doll's House*.

What, as Merton asks, "can we gain by sailing to the moon if we are not able to cross the abyss that separates us from ourselves?"

That abyss is what Gilgamesh attempted to cross through a literal journey. So too, we might add, did Columbus and Cortez and millions of others. It's that horror of Africa in Joseph Conrad's *Heart of Darkness,* and it's the chaos in Hemingway's world outside that clean well-lighted tavern. For many Americans it's the emptiness of the continent itself—or it's the wolf and bear, the Indian, the Afro-American, the Chicano, the communist, the homosexual. For a woman it's the man, and for a man it's the woman.

The imagination tells us that another approach to the Other, to the wild, is to *enter* it. In doing so we discover that what gets transformed is not the other, but us—or, more simply, our very notion of otherness, which is healed even as we give ourselves over to what we have most deeply feared.

This, I believe, is at the heart of most rites of passage, from tribal initiations to Bar Mitzvahs and baptisms, and is, at heart, what is missing from many of our lives. We are missing ritual, ceremony, story. We are missing the poetry of our lives.

We are starving the imagination.

I want, in what follows, to find a way to give some food to the imagination. I want to come to this idea of the wild—this rapture of the deep—through stories of my own, but also through the exploration of key components of wildness as we experience it in literature and music and art, in sexuality, in pain and in love. I want to taste wildness, digest it, and let it digest me.

I want to let wildness eat my words.

13

Rapture of the Deep

At some point, all these stories teach us, our attempt to hold onto what we already know keeps us from growing. Our map keeps us imprisoned in ways of living that we learned as children. It kept us safe for a time—and may once have been a matter of sheer survival—but it also has kept us from knowing the actual thing itself. It has kept us from life.

I see this continually in my students, as I've seen it in my own life. They come in with beautifully detailed maps which help them place everything they experience: Christian and non-Christian, liberal and conservative, all the boundary lines perfectly clear and well policed.

And then they hit the literature classes. Or philosophy. Or religion, where the Bible itself is unpacked, historicized, rendered far more complicated as a usable map. As is that final touchstone of the evangelical, one's own "personal experience with Christ."

Ironically enough, at some point we discover that it is our very idea of Christ (or Buddha or Yahweh) that keeps us from the wildness that Christ in fact is. But we cannot trust ourselves to this pathless way. Outside this old story everything grows too dark.

Too often I see my students, as I see myself, wanting to remain children even as we know too much to ever go back, and even as we hunger for real life, the straight truth, which inevitably involves embracing this boundaryless way. In short, we wish to remain adolescents.

In the end, I believe, it is adolescence that has America enchanted. We long for true initiation, true surrender and depth—we long for that rapture—and yet we fear to step over the edge. We fear the dark that surrounds us in that wilderness. We have been taught well these past two hundred years; our history is the history of the Enlightenment, and we are Enlightenment's children, Enlightenment's favorite pupil: democracy and public education flow from it, along with capitalism and the achievements of science. America stands as a witness to Enlightenment's power, which is the power of the rational intellect as it distances and abstracts itself from the world around it.

Education: from the Latin *educare,* to lead forth, as on a road.

This is the power of law, of human justice and the courts. It is the power that decided in 1954 that segregation in the schools is unconstitutional, that it inherently undermines the essential right of all citizens to a decent and equal education.

Introduction

This is a beautiful and powerful tool. And yet, as we learned in Little Rock and a thousand other places, it is not a power that alone can change hearts.

Enlightenment, Western style, has been a road. It will continue, I'm sure, to be a road. It will not alone, however, carry us from adolescence into adulthood. It will not carry us through that wilderness because by definition it only knows how to define, which means to put boundaries around something. It knows how to limit, to classify, categorize, and analyze. It does not know how to *enter* the wild.

The history of the "development" of the American west is the best proof of that fact.

We have known how to tame wilderness, to analyze and transform it. As so many Westerns have taught us, we have traded in our guns for the law only to find that the gun remains as a final solution, whether this is in our high schools or in the Balkans.

In this way at least the Puritans and their descendants were right: none of this has brought us to what we truly set out to find, which was not security but our souls.

We have not known how to be wild. As a result we have, like Victor Frankenstein, created a monster.

Let me end here with one final example of our situation, and of its possible solution. In his autobiography *Of Water and the Spirit*, the African writer Malidome Somé tells the story of his early life in a small village in western Africa, of his abduction, at the age of seven, by French missionaries, and of his subsequent education among the French over the next ten years—years in which, quite literally, he experienced first hand the end of a tribal way of thinking and the birth, through the gifts of writing and reading, of our way in the West. He then describes his escape from the missionary and his return home to a place where he is no longer known, and where he no longer knows himself.[22]

As a group of Cambodian refugees put it, "we survived the torture by letting our souls leave our bodies; now they are gone and we do not know where they are."

In Somé's case the torture was itself a kind of separating of soul from body: it was a crash course in western dualism.

He has, as his family tells him, lost his soul. And they are not speaking figuratively: they mean that he truly has lost something essential to his being. The elders decide that for him to return he must attempt to go through *baor*, initiation. The heart of his book is the description of this experience, which amounts to, in short, an end to one way of education and the beginning of another. But in this latter method there are no clear roads. The education of initiation is *guided*—there are elders present with the youths—but in some essential sense there is no definable way. And this is the essence *of* the education: it comes *because* there is no road. As his father tells him, "knowing what Baor is will not protect you. It will only save you from being initiated. This is not what you need. You cannot want Baor and protection at the same time. The very reason you need Baor is because you grew up protected. Protection is toxic to the person being safeguarded. . . . When you protect something, the thing you are keeping safe decays."

There are no Cliff Notes here, his father is saying to him—only the cliff itself.

I teach this book at the university where I am a professor. I teach it as a supplement (or challenge) to the very style of education that the students are acquiring and that I of course am teaching—that Western Enlightenment from which Somé fled. I teach it as a challenge to the definition of Christianity and "salvation" that most of these students have inherited from their families and their churches. And yet I also try to suggest that at the very heart of this initiation is a process, a *way*, that in fact should be utterly familiar to the Christian. What Somé experiences is exactly what Jesus experienced in the wilderness, what the Jews experienced in their Exodus across the desert, and what we are invited to experience in our own lives. It is not a permanent loss of the tools of the Enlightenment (Somé did, after all, go onto doctorate degrees in both France and the U.S., and he wrote this book) but it is, at a profound level, an entry back into a way that is found only through surrendering all the tools we spend such effort developing in our students.

The chapter I always invite my students to read is called "In the Arms of the Green Lady." Here Somé describes a moment early in his initiation: he is invited to sit before a tree and stare at it until "something happens." It is, from a western perspective, an exercise in futility.

Introduction

What can happen? As Somé himself says, he can analyze the tree, categorize it, compare it, draw it; he could figure out ways to put it to use; he could even *fantasize* about it: he could make something up *as if* he were really seeing something there, as if imagination were simply a matter of fiction.

He could, in other words, begin to lie. Which is precisely what he does, to the horror and shock of the elders who know (in ways that mystify Somé) that he *is* lying.

Curiously, it is precisely at this point—when he has, apparently, run out of options—that a genuine shift begins to occur. Significantly it begins with a movement that seems absurd to our western ears: he begins to talk to the tree as if, he says, "I had finally discovered that it had a life of its own."

He is now standing at the crossroads where two different ideas of education meet. Here, of course, is precisely where Hermes is to be found: it's the boundary (among other things) between adolescence and adulthood. But if we think of the development of analytical skills as the goal of the mature educated adult, we are invited to think again—or to *stop* thinking and to become again as a child. This is an initiation into a place that much of our culture no longer even imagines. It requires throwing out the map handed down to him and trusting another way where analysis can no longer guide him.

At this point he's on his own: he's in the dark woods, up mutation's creek. And yet, mysteriously, by arriving at this dead end, this place where all his attempts at control fail him, he's able to experience what I would call grace. He surrenders, or is surrendered, and finds himself stepping off the old road and into something dark, something impossible, and something unutterably beautiful:

> Suddenly there was a flash in my spirit like mild lightning, and a cool breeze ran down my spine and into the ground where I had been sitting for the past one and a half days. My entire body felt cool. The sun, the forest, and the elders and I understood that I was in another reality, witnessing a miracle. All the trees around my yila were glowing like fires or breathing lights. I felt weightless, as if I were at the center of a universe where everything was looking at me as if I were naked, weak, and innocent. For a moment I experienced a deep fear that I imagined was similar to what one feels when one is told that death is inevitably on its way. Indeed, I thought I was dead.

When he looks again, the tree is not a tree, but a woman in black. She lifts her veil, and he sees that her body is filled from the inside with a green light. Somé writes, "I do not know how I know this, but this green was the expression of immeasurable love."

Whenever I teach this book I always have at least one student ask whether I believe that what Somé describes "really" happened. I have, of course, no way of "really" knowing, and I say this to my students. He calls his book an autobiography, and so we are left with three possibilities: he might be lying, he might be deluded, or he might be telling the truth. We are left to make up our own minds. To me what matters in this is being confronted by the possibility that he *might be telling the truth*. For my conservative students that is a wilderness indeed. I want my students to walk into that wilderness, just as I would want them to walk into the true wilderness that is everywhere in the Gospels, in the *Tao Te Ching*, in the work of Rumi and in the *Bhagavad Gita*. I want us to go where Gilgamesh failed to go.

It may be, such texts are telling us, that there is a road that is no road, a road that is nothing other than reality itself—a road that we are invited not to walk but to become. To *be*.

For me, for whatever biological and cultural and family reasons, this has always been the only important moment. Dostoyevsky understood this, as did Flannery O'Connor, who writes that "reality is something to which we must be returned at considerable cost."

It is not, finally, a question of safety. It's a question of a heart on fire. And when this is the case there is no choice but to spend a lifetime seeking ways to put it out—or else to let it burn, like a beautiful tongue of flame.

Introduction

NOTES

1 Leslie Silko, *Ceremony* (New York: Viking, 1977) p. 260.

2 *Gilgamesh*, translated by David Ferry (New York: Farrar, Strauss & Giroux, 1992).

3 Thompson, *The Time Falling Bodies Take to Light* (New York: St. Martin's Press, 1981) p. 203.

4 Linda Gregg, interviewed in *Poets and Writers* November 1991.

5 Robert Hass, "Images," in *Twentieth Century Pleasures* (New York: Echo Press, 1984), p. 275.

6 Laurence Van Der Post, "Wilderness—A Way of Truth," in *A Testament to the Wilderness: Ten Essays on an Address by C. A. Meier* (Santa Monica: Lapis Press, 1985), p. 47.

7 Stephen Levine, *Who Dies* (New York: Anchor Books, 1982), pp. 27-28.

8 Gary Snyder, *Practice of the Wild,* (San Francisco: North Point Press, 1990), p. 10. By definition the wild cannot be defended since definition means (by definition) to set limits to something, and the wild is precisely that which is without limits. And so any definition of the wild is by definition not the wild, since the wild will always exceed the boundaries of the definition. As Wallace Stevens says, the squirming facts exceed the squamous mind.

9 On mutation and evolution, see *The Universe Story* (Harper San Francisco 1992), p. 88. Thoreau's reading of Darwin brought him to similar insights, as Thoreau's biographer suggests. "Change, individuation, metamorphosis, transmigration of form all these pointed toward growth itself, not the grown thing, as the great underlying reality in nature." Robert D. Richardson Jr., *Henry Thoreau. A Life of the Mind* (Berkeley: University of California Press, 1986), p. 245.

10 Lewis Hyde, *Trickster Makes this World* (New York: North Point Press, 1998), pp. 6, 9, 137. See also the conversation between video artist (and trickster) Bill Viola and Lewis Hyde in *Bill Viola* (New York: Whiney Museum of American Art, 1998). pp. 151-2.

11 Lao Tzo's *Taoteching*, translated by Red Pine (San Francisco: Mercury House Press, 1996), p. 22.

12 John(Fire) Lame Deer and Richard Erdoes, *Lame Deer, Seeker of Visions* (New York: Simon & Schuster, 1972), pp. 276-7.

13 Wendell Berry, *Home Economics* (San Francisco: North Point Press, 1987), pp. 143-4.

14 Chuang Tzu, *Basic Writings*, translated by Burton Watson (New York: Columbia University Press, 1964) p.127.

15 Charles E. Winquist, *Homecoming: Interpretation, Transformation and Individuation* (Missoula: Scholar's Press 1978), p.80.

16 Vicki Hearne, *Adam's Task: Calling Animals By Name* (New York: Knopf, 1987) p.140, 154.

17 From Coleridge's *Philosophical Lectures* (1818), quoted by Richard Haven in *Patterns of Consciousness: An Essay on Coleridge* (University of Massachusetts Press, 1969, p. 173.

18 Quoted in *"Not Laws of Nature but Li (Pattern) of Nature"* by Delores LaChapelle, in *The Wilderness Condition*, edited by Max Oelschlaeger (San Francisco: Sierra Club Books, 1992), p.225.

19 Milosz to Merton in *Striving Towards Being: The Letters of Thomas Merton and Czeslaw Milosz,* edited by Robert Faggen (New York: Farrar, Strauss & Giroux, 1997), p.39.

20 Thich Nhat Hanh, *The Heart of Understanding: Commentaries on the Prajnaparamita Heart Sutra* (Berkeley: Parallax Prss) p. 15.

21 Thomas Merton, *The Wisdom of the Desert* (New Directions, 1960), pp 5-7.

22 Malidome Somé, *Of Water and the Spirit* (Putnam 1994). It's worth comparing Somé's experience with that of Isaac McCaslin in William Faulkner's *The Bear.* As a boy Ike wishes to get a glimpse of the famous patriarch of the woods, the bear Old Ben, who comes to represent the wilderness, an untainted connection to the land. He fails, however, until he listens to the words of Sam, the son of a

Introduction

Chickasaw chief and so himself, in this context, a close connection to an older way of being, " 'It's the gun,' Sam said.... 'The gun. You will have to choose.'" And so he leaves the gun behind and heads farther into the woods, only to find that even this was not enough. As Faulkner puts it:

> He had already relinquished, of his will, because of his need, in humility and peace and without regret, yet apparently that had not been enough, the leaving of the gun was not enough. He stood for a moment-a child, alien and lost in the green and soaring gloom of the markless wilderness. Then he relinquished completely to it. It was the watch and the compass. He was still tainted. He removed the linked chain of the one and the looped thong of the other from his overalls and hung them on a bush and leaned the stick beside them and entered it.

That linked chain becomes an image of all that gives us guidance through this wilderness. As Isaac discovers, however, the chain binds him down; it blocks his ability to enter more deeply into the wild and thus see the beautiful thing itself. His desire for entry into this reality is greater than his fear of being lost in it.

CHAPTER ONE

Pitched at the Brink

A religious devotion to the truth, to the splendor of the authentic, involves the writer in a process rewarding in itself; but when that devotion brings us to undreamed abysses and we find ourselves sailing slowly over them and landing on the other side—that's ecstasy.
—Denise Levertov[1]

Early one morning, after four days of hiking and camping on and off the Pacific Crest Trail in the North Cascades, my eight-year-old daughter awoke tired and cross. I was outside the tent, a hundred yards to the east, close to where the trail crossed the meadows, where we'd watched the black bear browsing among the huckleberries the evening before. But such delights were now forgotten. I heard howls from within the tent—protests. Never mind that John Muir called what we were doing sauntering; Katie wanted none of it.

We were, I thought, alone in the area, meaning there were no other humans around. Miles from a road, isolated between the ridges at Macalaster Pass, the sound of my daughter's cries seemed to volley down and across the mountains all the way to Stehekin.

And then return. Only this time the howls weren't from Katie but from wolves—two or three or more—over the next ridge to the east. The cries were deep and long, mournful, haunting.

The wolves sang for five minutes. I listened, standing alone in the meadow, watching the light inch its way over the landscape. Deer prints were visible on the trail before my feet. Wildflowers blazed around me. Rainbow Creek carried glacial debris for miles down to Lake Chelan, a dozen miles below us.

I remember this moment nine months later as I stand on my front porch and watch my daughter walk down the sidewalk, lunch box in hand, to her carpool. She turns, smiles and waves, then vanishes from my sight.

I remember too that a mile farther down the hill an old friend of mine is dying. Yesterday I sat beside her as she refused again to eat, muttering in semi-conscious frenzy, *it's wrong, it's wrong*. I read to her even as she slept, moving far beyond my words. A hundred yards below us Puget Sound remained calm, unruffled by the rage that continued to burn inside her.

Something true ties us all together—my friend, the wolves, my daughter; it's the face of death, and the honesty and freedom this allows. Wolves do not wear masks. Neither do children. Neither does death.

It is beauty I am seeing, as strange as that may sound. I grieve for my dying friend, and yet I see this beauty. I see it so deeply I want to dance around her, to rouse her to its splendor. For they—both my friend and death—are my teachers.

So, too, my daughter. The braided girl who runs off to join her friends has sung with wolves. In hearing her song I learned this truth: a beautiful darkness, a wildness, runs between them. Invisible threads link us all, like the mycorrhizae that weave together the roots of trees beneath the forest floor.

Wilderness is not what I once imagined. I was trained by early twentieth-century literature to see little in nature but chaos and dark disorder. In Joseph Conrad, for example, civilization forms a thin veneer of artificial light over the great horror, that heart of darkness which is both his image of Africa and, more deeply, of the Godless void at the heart of everything. So, too, in Hemingway, whose boyhood home I used to walk by on my way home from school. His image of the tent along the river and the clean, well-lit cafe become signs of home-as-we-make-it, fragile barriers against the intruding emptiness.

It is in part the apparent lack of pattern, the feeling of unpredictability that appalls us. We fear both the failure of control (for without pattern we cannot tell where things are going) and the failure of meaning, since we discover meaning through pattern. We feel exposed in nature partly because of this possibility of the unpredictable, and we spend an enormous amount of time and energy trying to con-

A vulnerability

trol it. This process in us may even mark the turning point in human culture: from the Paleolithic hunter-gatherer who primarily followed the food source, to the Neolithic farmer cultivator who began to shape that source to meet his own ends.

And yet we find beauty not simply in a static order, but—in the words of Gert Eilenberger, a German physicist—in "dynamical systems. Our feeling for beauty is inspired by the harmonious arrangement of order and disorder as it occurs in natural objects—in clouds, trees, mountain ranges, or snow crystals. The shapes of all these are dynamical processes jelled into physical forms, and particular combinations of order and disorder are typical for them."

As one ideal defines beauty (and the divine) as static and fixed, another defines these in terms of flow: "shape plus change, motion plus form." Flow assumes "that change in systems reflected some reality independent of the particular instant." This, I see, is the essence of chaos: "a delicate balance between forces of stability and forces of instability." Flow sees pattern in process; it makes connections in the midst of the apparently disconnected.

D'Arcy Thompson gets close to this understanding of flow. His unique book, *On Growth and Form*, was extravagantly praised by Sir Peter Medawar as "beyond comparison the finest work of literature in all the annals of science that have been recorded in the English tongue." James Gleich summarizes:

> [Thompson] thought of life as life, always in motion, always responding to rhythms—the "deep-seated rhythms of growth" which he believed created universal forms. He considered his proper study not just the material forms of things but their dynamics— "the interpretation, in terms of force, of the operations of Energy." He was enough of a mathematician to know that cataloguing shapes proved nothing. But he was enough of a poet to trust that neither accident nor purpose could explain the striking universality of forms he had assembled in his long years of gazing at nature. Physical laws must explain it, governing force and growth in ways that were just out of understanding's reach. . . . Behind the particular, visible shapes of matter must lie ghostly forms serving as invisible templates. Forms in motion.[2]

Back in my study, losing my daughter's figure in the flow of traffic below me on Third Avenue, I stare out the window as other neighborhood kids walk past. They are eyeballed by the black crows perched high above on telephone wires, appropriating, as is the crow's way, anything to their use. Below them the ivy, introduced to the region by white settlers a hundred years ago, climbs and covers the cherry stump, its voracious growth almost visible to my gaze. Like humans, ivy doesn't wait for an invitation.

Forms in motion. I listen to Dvorak's *Slavonic Dances* as the wind plays and as butterflies rise and fall above the roses outside my window. The Butterfly Effect, I suddenly remember: the tiny stir of air in Seattle today that transforms storm systems tomorrow in New York. Nothing stays put, or disconnected.

I pull out a book of essays—Denise Levertov's old *The Poet in the World*—and begin to read. Piano in the background. My dog stretches and slides his black body illicitly three-quarters of the way across the living room couch. I read by the light from the study window—a gray, overcast morning.

"Back of the idea of organic form," Levertov wrote some thirty years ago, "is the concept that there is a form in all things (and in our experience) which the poet can discover and reveal." It is "an intuition of an order, a form beyond forms in which forms partake."[3] Inconceivable because it is beyond conception—and yet it is the very heart of conception.

"Where true 'free verse' is concerned with the maintenance of its freedom from all bonds," Levertov writes, "'organic' poetry, having freed itself from imposed forms, voluntarily places itself under other laws: the variable, unpredictable, but nonetheless strict laws of inscape, discovered by instress. Its discipline begins with the development of the utmost attentiveness. . . ."[4]

Gerard Manley Hopkins most likely derived the term inscape from the model of "landscape," "seascape." "Scape" is a suffix linked with the etymologically related suffix "-ship," used to indicate the creation, meaning, or condition of a thing. "Landscape," then, would suggest the meaning or condition—the essential quality—of land. "Inscape" is the condition of in-ness: a way of knowing the innerness of a thing. It is full entry into the other. Hopkins, in his journal, gives a simple example: "I do not think I have ever seen anything more beautiful than the bluebell I have been looking at. I know the beauty of our Lord by it. Its inscape is mixed of strength and grace. . . ."

Inscape incarnates being. Yet the pattern which reveals inscape in any particular object is not static but dynamic; inscape is energy. Our work is to know it and to incarnate it ourselves in the mess and struggle—the chaos—of our own lives. And to do this, we must listen—we must listen hard. This holds true whether we are poets, potters, teachers, or parents. We listen to where that still, small voice within is leading us. And for most of us at the end of the twentieth century, the shape our life takes is not a sonnet. Nothing so clear and so formal will do.

So, too, must the poet see. "The forms more apt to express the sensibility of our age are the exploratory, open ones," Levertov continues, in a later essay. "Such poetry . . . incorporates and reveals the process of thinking/feeling, feeling/thinking, rather than focusing more exclusively on its results. . . . And the crucial precision tool for creating this exploratory mode is the line break."[5]

The linebreak? I suddenly recall two lines from Eliot: "Words, after speech, reach / into the silence. . . ." This silence of the line-break itself teaches us how to hear. It is akin to a still moment in the woods: we attend, stretch toward (*ad-tendere*) the silence. We listen like deer.

Even the simple slash (/) between these lines conveys something of this power. These breaks, I realize, are the cliff's edge of art, profound and yet as subtle as the pulse of an artery.

In poetry, words reach—and for the slightest moment nothing is there. Words . . . reach / into the silence. They seek this silence because it is their source, and they seem to find it only by trying to leap out of their skin. Words in a poem move like a shedding snake, only for the poem there is no visible skin beneath—no sound, just a "spiritual body."

Words, like each of us, must become that toward which they long. Words must become their own opposite, their shadow, silence.

I return to Levertov, this time to her poems. I'm looking for a favorite of mine from *A Door in the Hive*, "The Blind Man's House at the Edge of the Cliff."

Pitched at the Brink

At the jutting rim of the land he lives,
but not from ignorance,
not from despair.
He knows one extra step from his seaward
wide-open door would be
a step into salt air,
and he has no longing to shatter himself
far below, where the breakers
grind granite to sand.
No, he has chosen a life pitched at the brink, a nest on the swaying
tip of a branch, for good reason:

dazzling within his darkness
is the elusive deep horizon. Here
nothing intrudes, palpable shade,
between his eager
inward gaze
and the vast enigma.
If he could fly he would drift forever
into that veil, soft and receding.

He knows that if he could see
he would be no wiser.
High on the windy cliff he breathes
face to face with desire.[6]

Each line in this poem is exploratory. It's a kind of precipice, marked in the enjambed lines, where there is no tiny black comma holding us in place at the end. We go over the edge, hanging in the thin air of silence before breath and pitch pick us up below.

While the poem is, I think, about the contemplative life—this blind hermit living at the edge is each of us, potentially—it does more: it enacts the contemplative. Its own wildness is created within the deep freedom of poetic discipline.

Levertov finds the jutting rim of the poem and the rifts that lie within. That's the feel of the long first line jutting out, and of the other lines that seem to end in midair. This is the place the poem inhabits. Its freedom is created in its precarious balance between rim and open air, between words and blank space.

It's almost impossible to describe how lovely this is—the blind man's and the poet's choices to bring us to this "life / pitched at the brink." The lines carry us right to the edge, but always with a sense of balance and control. They are both pitched and nested, at home and in flight—the perfect image of the contemplative. This, every syllable proclaims, is the diamond of the disciplined life; in its rare beauty, its wildness and control, it enacts what it describes.

~

I take a break, pour a cup of tea, and put on Schubert's *String Quintet in C Major*, stunned as the Allegro springs forth. The interplay between the additional cello and the first violin, where notes are sustained, suspended, as others play and leap about, around and over—it all seems, like the Levertov poem, deeply balanced and yet at risk: exploratory, like any great art.

The music and poem play off one another in my heart and mind, both changing the look and feel of the world outside my window, a world dancing to the same wind that blows through Schubert and Levertov. Everywhere life sways to this breeze, this deep underlying rhythm which manifests itself in so many forms: waves of the ocean, scarred rock face in the mountains, poetry and music. These forms bend like plants to the light, but arise out of a kind of darkness—an unspeakable mystery, beautiful, unpredictable, unknown.

It is toward this mystery, both dark and light, that Levertov's hermit (and the poem itself) moves, even as he arises from it. It is not simply out there; "dazzling within his darkness" the poet tells us, "is the elusive deep horizon."

Some years ago, in a late-evening phone call, Denise reminded me of lines from Henry Vaughan: "There is in God, (some say), / A deep but dazzling darkness, as men here / Say it is late and dusky, because they / See not all clear. . . ."[7] Again the Butterfly Effect: across three hundred years, the small stir of air in these words reappears, transformed.

"Dazzle" arises from "daze": to stun, stupefy; to dim the vision blind with intense light (its root is **dhe*: to vanish). My mind flits back to John of the Cross: "When the divine light of contemplation strikes souls not yet entirely illumined, it causes spiritual darkness, for it not only surpasses them but also deprives and darkens their act of understanding. This is why St. Dionysus and other mystical theologians call this infused contemplation a ray of darkness; that is, for the soul not yet illumined and purged. For this great supernatural light overwhelms the intellect...."[8]

The hermit is the contemplative who removes all barriers between himself and the infinite horizon within. Like Gloucester in King Lear, he is brought to the very edge—but that edge is where he must live. To leap is to plummet. He has carried himself as far as he can go.

It's morning still, the house is quiet, and by now the sun, concealed by the clouds, will have reached the garden, rising in its arc over the top of the huge maple that shades much of the front yard and sidewalk. But until just now, listening to the music, I've noticed little of this. I've been inside, marking the verse's time and sound, finding connections, and just listening. This act has carried me closer to some edge in myself—the point where understanding leaves off. Analysis brings me to the borders of meaning, of what can be understood of a poem's order. But true order goes deeper into places I can no longer track. This is where the path ends.

This, I see now, is not a poem of fulfillment. It is instead a poem that carries us to the edge of fulfillment—or to where desire itself seems to be a kind of fulfillment, a place where we long only for more of this dazzling darkness, even while we are held back by the restraints of poetic form itself. We are both brought deep and held by discipline: the discipline of the poem, and thus of the poet.

This same discipline and desire, I sense, is what carried the Chinese poet Han Shan to Cold Mountain—and, even more profoundly, turned Han Shan into Cold Mountain.

> Men these days search for a way through the clouds,
> But the cloud way is dark and without sign.
> The mountains are high and often steep and rocky;
> In the broadest valleys the sun seldom shines.
> Green crests before you and behind,
> White clouds to east and west—
> Do you want to know where the cloud way lies?
> There it is, in the midst of the Void![9]

The cloud is often a symbol of this apophatic way; as anyone who has hiked at high elevations knows, to go this way is to give up direction. The path is there, and you may even be on it, but you cannot know that through your senses. The way of the cloud is the way without a way.

Here, the mystic Jan van Ruusbroec writes,

> There is a blissful crossing over and a self-transcending immersion into a state of essential bareness, where all the divine names and modes and all the living ideas which are reflected in the mirror of divine truth all pass away into simple ineffability without mode and without reason. . . . This is that modeless being which all fervent interior spirits have chosen above all things, that dark stillness in which all lovers lose their way.[10]

Face to face with desire: there is, the poem suggests, nowhere else to go. "I am on the very edge, sir," the shepherd says to Oedipus, who loses and gains himself in the very same instant. "We are both on the edge," Oedipus replies. "Dazzling within his darkness / is the elusive deep horizon."

So often in meditation, in the practice of an art, or in the wilderness, we approach something so honest, so touched with life, that we are startled, dazzled by its splendor and by what it reveals. It is like sitting in the presence of a dying friend: all façades are down, and we feel a startling freedom, a gift in arriving at last at a kind of truth. A tremendous vista opens within and before us; we know that to enter it fully requires from us as well a death.

Wordsworth knew such moments as a child, and they awed him: he describes reaching out to touch a tree just to assure himself of something solid, something other. And yet such intimations also marked his future gift as a visionary poet.

It's not surprising that many of this poet's greatest moments come on cliffs. "Tintern Abbey," for example: "Once again," he writes, "do I behold these steep and lofty cliffs, / That on a wild secluded scene impress / Thoughts of more deep seclusion; and connect / The landscape with the quiet of the sky."

Herein is a continual interchange between the mind and this wild scene. Like the mind, the cliffs themselves are a power: mind and cliffs marry, as seeing leads to nature's acting on the mind, and thus to the mind's perception of ultimate connection.

And, of course, this is not all. These cliffs live in the memory; to them the poet owes that serene and blessed mood

> In which the affections gently lead us on—
> Until, the breath of this corporeal frame
> And even the motion of our human blood
> Almost suspended, we are laid asleep
> In body, and become a living soul:
> While with an eye made quiet by the power
> Of harmony, and the deep power of joy,
> We see into the life of things.

This is as precise a description of movement into the contemplative as poetry is likely to give us. Breath—even blood—seems suspended, hung in the air. In body we are "laid asleep" while we become—haunting phrase—a "living soul."

"Do not suppose," writes the anonymous author of *The Cloud of Unknowing*, "that because I have spoken of darkness and of a cloud I have in mind the clouds you see in an overcast sky or the darkness of your house when your candle fails."

> If I had, you could with a little imagination picture the summer skies breaking through the clouds or a clear light brightening the dark winter. But this isn't what I mean at all so forget this sort of nonsense. When I speak of darkness, I mean the absence of knowledge. If you are not able to understand something or if you have forgotten it, are you not in the dark as regards this thing? You cannot see it with your mind's eye. Well, in the same way, I have not said "cloud" but cloud of unknowing. For it is a darkness of unknowing that lies between you and your God.[11]

Compare this to the famous passage in Wordsworth's *Prelude*, as the author, on his walking tour through the Alps, learns to his dismay that he has already crossed the peaks. "I was lost," he writes, "Halted without an effort to break through." The confusion in this passage is palpable: he had reached the heights without knowing it. No celestial rose, no illumination. So what was the point of the journey? Only now, years later, as Wordsworth composes this scene anew, does the meaning break in upon him:

> Imagination—here the Power so called
> Through sad incompetence of human speech,
> That awful Power rose from the mind's abyss
> Like an unfathered vapour that enwraps,
> At once, some lonely traveller.

For Wordsworth it is the imagination itself, "that power from the Mind's abyss," which takes over the senses: "but with a flash that has revealed / The invisible world." Darkness descends upon the intellect with a flash. Just here, in this force that defies analysis, do we reach our unexpected end. We discover that our heart and home

> Is with infinitude, and only there;
> With hope it is, hope that can never die,
> Effort, and expectation, and desire,
> And something evermore about to be.[12]

Effort, expectation, and desire: even as Wordsworth was led as both pilgrim and poet, so too are we led through the poem, even through analysis, to that "something. . . ."

While analysis may glorify the separation it imposes between myself and what I study, it may also lead me deeply into that subject. Analysis may lead me beyond itself, and thus beyond myself.

At the heart of this whole issue is the question of naming. We enter the world by naming it. We may have begun this practice to establish power and control (which is one reading of the Genesis story), but we may also name because we seek a lost intimacy. To name my region's birds, its trees and rocks and flowers, is a way back into a relationship from which I've been separated since (at least) my birth into language.

Yet at some point this way of knowing ends. We experience something that transcends the old split between subject and object, between reader and poem. And something else arises: a sense of beauty which doesn't just see meaning in the connections but moves inside and makes love, taking pointless, aimless delight. We enter the dance.

In poetry, as in meditation, we no longer study the mountain; like Han Shan, we find ourselves as mountain.

Or like Li Po, who writes, *We sit together, the mountain and me / until only the mountain remains.*[13]

It is to this same place, at his precarious best, that Wordsworth leads me, and it is why I go on reading him. Sheer beauty: beauty so sublime that the body cannot contain it except by dissolving into that which it loves. Call it that indefinable something more that he knew, witnessed, and reached in his effortless iambics—a rhythm that matched his long, contemplative striding over the Grasmere hills. He walks and writes for that awe-filled moment when the senses go out and darkness comes on with a flash.

As Wordsworth describes his descent to Chamonix, we move from the quick journal-like descriptions, told in relatively flat language, into a sentence seventeen lines long, in words as paradoxical as any Zen master's—or any physicists. Eternal process is what he sees; forms in motion: "The immeasurable height / Of woods decaying, never to be decayed, / The stationary blasts of waterfalls. . . ." Endless conflict that is somehow still "the workings of one mind. . . ."

It's now early afternoon; for a few more hours I'm alone. Out the window, somewhere behind the cumulus clouds to the west, rise the Olympics. To the east lie the Cascades, part of a more or less continuous mountain chain extending for 1,700 miles from Northern California to Alaska. I'm in between, in the valley once covered by glaciers. This hill on which my house momentarily rests is supported by 3,000 feet of glacial deposits.

"Nowhere do the mountain masses and peaks present such strange, fantastic, dauntless and startling outlines as here," Henry Custer wrote in 1859 when working his way through the North Cascades for (deep irony!) the International Boundary Commission. Boundaries? Those that do exist—between water and land, between rock and animal—are to the geologic eye all too transient; inevitably the one flows into the other.

There are still areas of back country that have yet to feel the imprint of a human foot. A certain silence exists up there, a dry stillness in the summer months, smelling of pine and wildflowers. Aster, lupine, American bistort bloom on the slopes in the late spring sun, spring coming to some places in late July. Marmot and mule deer, white-tailed ptarmigan; forests of western red cedar and Douglas fir; deep glaciers scored by crevasses; permanent snowfields.

There is a kind of romance to it all, especially when viewed from the distance of the city. But romance has a way of turning as a relationship becomes intimate. It's the stillness when the sun falls—the wind dying, birdcalls suddenly expiring. And the immense dark.

I discovered this for myself a few years back when I went up into the Cascades alone, after having been away from the mountains for five years. It was mid-October, in the midst of some of the worst flooding the area had known. I was there, like Wordsworth, both fleeing and seeking. I wanted what I couldn't have and so sought in the mountains the emptiness I'd already been given.

It rained as soon as I reached the boundary of Mount Baker National Park. It kept raining as I sat in the car at the trailhead and ate my lunch, and continued raining as I changed into my boots, got out, pulled the pack from the back seat, and hoisted it upon me. The rain grew heavy as I walked; I felt pregnant with it for five long miles.

The rain seemed endless, permanent. I knew it had preceded me and would be there after I left—would return and be there like those mountains, sister to those great cliffs, a part of that landscape which people here learn to live within and love. I had forgotten about rain, how after a while it exposes you, gets into everything you wear, everything you are. There's no hiding from it. You toss aside the umbrella and face whatever it is that wears you down.

I reached Goat Lake in mid-afternoon, ate, looked around at the small pools of water at the campsites, at the quickly shortening day, and made a decision: throwing the pack over my shoulders I started back down the five-mile trail.

Not far from the lake was a plateau where the path had drowned itself in large puddles. I forgot about the turn it took and walked instead straight down toward a raging Elliot Creek. When I reached it I knew I had gone wrong, and so I hiked back up the hill, only to find myself once more at the campsites at Goat Lake. I stopped, turned around, and went back down, searching for some sign of the way out. I looked at the puddles, which said nothing, and looked up toward the mist hovering over the cliffs. Then I looked down toward the creek, which I knew could take me back home in a hurry.

I learned that five miles could be a long way when you've managed to lose yourself. There was a lot of unknown space to cross. Rifts. So I walked, trying to understand what couldn't be understood. Damp all the way through, made more vulnerable by the weather closing in on me, the fog drifting farther down the mountain, the trees utterly silent and unconcerned—I was alone, absolutely, and for the moment I could do nothing about it except to walk.

As I thought about a warm bath, a beer, music, and friends all somewhere far below, I realized that even there I would find no protection from this overawing solitude, this death I felt myself carrying down the mountain. I knew it in my bones: there is no way out.

Facing a slow death is a lot like walking in the rain with miles to go: you can curse it, fight it, try to cover yourself from it, try to ignore it—it won't make a lot of difference, not in the long run. So you might as well greet it. And for a time as I walked I found myself exuberantly crying, Let it come. Just let it come. Let the rain come. Let the monsters out.

I reached the car two hours later, and was home in two more. Pulled everything out again, spread the wet sleeping bag and tent on the floor by the heater, ate some of the food that belonged up on the mountain, and finally took a long, hot bath. The World Series was on the radio; Kirk Gibson homered for the Dodgers in the ninth an hour after I arrived.

We forget what mountains are like. Wordsworth wasn't kidding when he wrote about them breathing down his neck. They do breathe. They fill immensity.

※

The sun has briefly returned. I see my daughter struggling up the hill, her coat and sweater slung over her back, her blue lunch box in one hand which also clutches sheets of notes from school. I go outside into the light to meet her.

Katie wants to jump rope. I sit on the cool porch steps to watch her, then move to the large trunk of the old cherry tree that the previous owner had chopped down. I'm watching the light. At the corner of the house, the lilacs are out. Up the hill our friend Kathryn is hanging clothes on the line to dry. She takes advantage of the wind rolling down from the mountains, the western slope.

"The edge is what I have," I remember, still lost in the shadows of my past. There is this too—the madness that came to Theodore Roethke, who wrote that line not many miles from where I now sit. The madness was there in Hopkins as well: "Mind has mountains," he wrote, "cliffs of fall / Frightful, sheer, no-man-fathomed. Hold them cheap / May who ne'er hung there."[14]

I know something of this edge, this darkness too, even as I watch my daughter play. But today I wonder: perhaps that darkness is simply life bursting up through the fissures of the world—and things dying to make way. Perhaps this is what we mean by sacrifice: *sacer* + *facere*; to make sacred. This is the dazzling darkness at the heart of love.

We go inside, and when Katie goes upstairs I return to my desk. On impulse I pull out Peter Matthiessen's *The Snow Leopard*, searching for a passage about the mountains, something I first read a dozen years ago in *The New Yorker* and found again when I took the book with me on retreat to the monastery in Snowmass. After a few minutes I find what I'm looking for: Matthiessen is on his way down from the Himalayas, having missed (like Wordsworth) almost everything he'd thought he'd come to find, including the snow leopard itself. He is at Shay, the high point of his trip, but is preparing to leave. It's November 15, 1973.

> Near my lookout, I find a place to meditate, out of the wind, a hollow on the ridge where snow has melted. My brain soon clears in the cold mountain air, and I feel better. Wind, blowing grasses, sun: the dying grass, the notes of southbound birds in the mountain sky are no more fleeting than the rock itself, no more so and no less—all is the same. The mountain withdraws into its stillness, my body dissolves into the sunlight, tears fall that have nothing to do with "I." What it is that brings them on, I do not know.[15]

I finish reading, set down the book, and listen. No sound. The dog sleeps on the couch, my daughter reads or sews or draws upstairs, steadily growing into her own life. On my desk are the photographs from our trip just weeks ago to the Marble Mountain Wilderness in the Klamaths. I glance through them again, remembering in particular the long, hot climb we made one afternoon on Marble Rim, 7,000 feet up, resting briefly at the sheer edge of things. We watched as a red-tailed hawk soared far below. Down the valley, a tiny ribbon of water etched itself through the forest. Sun and sky and stillness, just for a moment. It was as far as we could go.

I do not know how this seemed to Katie, or how she will remember it in years to come. To me it was one of those moments, like the crying of the wolves, when wild called out to wild. It is a place that always beckons—a true place, a jutting rim where I momentarily perched on the edge of the possible.

On our way back down Katie began to teach me one of the songs she'd learned in choir, a simple hymn called "Joseph's Lullaby: "Dream your dreams of angels and light, / I'll be there throughout the long night / A man needs deep silence to feel such deep joy. . . ."

Beneath the brilliant sun she sang, and then I sang, haltingly following behind.

Notes

1 Denise Levertov, "Some Notes on Organic Form," *The Poet in the World* (New York: New Directions, 1973), p.13. This essay has been reprinted in *New & Selected Essays* (New York: New Directions, 1992), pp. 67–73.

2 The comments on Chaos theory here and below are primarily indebted to James Gleich's *Chaos: Making a New Science* (New York: Viking, 1987): p.117 (the words of Gert Eilenberger); p. 195 ("shape plus change,"); p. 309 (the definition of chaos); p. 202 (on D'Arcy Thompson) and 8 (the Butterfly Effect).

3 Levertov, "Some Notes on Organic form,' p. 7.

4 Levertov, "A Further Definition," in *The Poet in the World*, pp. 14–15.

5 Levertov, "On the Function of the Line," in *Light Up the Cave* (New York: New Directions, 1981), pp. 61–2. The essay is reprinted in *New & Selected Essays*, pp. 78–87.

6 *A Door in the Hive* (New York: New Directions, 1989), p. 10.

7 Henry Vaughan, "The Night," first published in 1655. See *The Complete Poems*, ed. Alan Rudrum (Penguin Books, 1976), p. 290.

8 John of the Cross, from *Dark Night of the Soul*, Book Two, Chapter Five. See *Light from Light: An Anthology of Christian Mysticism*, edited by Louis Dupre & James A. Wiseman, O.S.B. (Mahwah, NJ: Paulist Press, 1988), p. 305.

9 Han Shan, *Cold Mountain*, translated by Burton Watson (London: Jonathon Cape, 1970), p. 55.

10 Ruusbroec, *The Spiritual Espousals*, Book Three, Part Four, excerpted in *Light From Light*, p. 192.

11 *The Cloud of Unknowing*, edited by William Johnston (New York: Image Books, 1973), pp. 52–3.

12 Wordsworth, *The Prelude*, Book Six, lines 592–6, 605–608.

13 Li Po, translated by Sam Hamill. See *A Book of Luminous Things*, edited by Czeslaw Milosz (New York: Harcourt Brace, 1996), p. 277.

14 Roethke, "In A Dark Time" (see The *Collected Poems* (New York: Anchor Books, 1975), p. 231), a poem that owes something to St. John of the Cross and something more to Paul Tillich's *The Courage to Be*. The Hopkins quote is from his sonnet, "No Worst, There is None. . . ."

15 *The Snow Leopard* (New York: Viking, 1978), pp. 248–9.

Caspar David Freidrich, *Wanderer Abover the Mist*
(*Der Wanderer uber dem Nebelmeer*, 1817–18)

INTERLUDE

Caspar David Friedrich: Wanderer above the Mists

Stand on the peak of the mountain, contemplate the long ranges of hills, observe the courses of the rivers and all the glories offered to your view, and what feeling seizes you? It is a calm prayer, you lose yourself in unbounded space, your whole being undergoes a clarification and purification, your ego disappears, you are nothing, God is everything.

With this excerpt from the painter Carl Gustav Cams's *Letters on Landscape Painting* (1835) we come close to the spirit of both Wordsworth and to Caspar David Freidrich, whose *Wanderer Above the Mist (Der Wanderer uber dem Nebelmeer,* 1817–18) is reproduced here. Seeing this painting at the end of the twentieth century, however, gives us little idea of the radical nature of Friedrich's work, where for the first time in western art wilderness is explicitly equated with the holy space of the cathedral.

Hugh Honour, in his study of Romantic art, concisely compares Friedrich's departure with a painting of a similar wilderness scene that would have met contemporary standards for the "sublime" (and for good taste). Caspar Wolf's Lauterargletscher (1776) is "skillfully composed according to eighteenth century conventions:"

> Human figures set the scale, mark the perspective recession and provide a comforting contrast with the desolation of the scene. Apprehensive dogs indicate the terror of the bare mountain, but men are in command of the situation, apparently engaged in rational discussion of the beauties and wonders of nature: one of them has prudently provided himself with a parasol. It is an appealing picture, which might serve to illustrate many an eighteenth century account of Alpine travels, full of feeling for the sublime and reflecting enlightened intellectual curiosity in natural phenomena. But it contains no hint of what Coleridge was to call "inner goings-on," no suspicion of a profounder meaning, of "something far more deeply interfused."[1]

With *The Wanderer above the Mists* we are much closer to Wordsworth's sense of this "something interfused," and closer too to the contemplative vision described in *The Cloud of Unknowing*—only here we are not so much engulfed in mystery as on the very edge of it. Here, too, in this vision of viewer, mist and rising sun (similar to Wordsworth's Snowdon passage), the external landscape becomes a kind of emblem for an internal spiritual state. It is clear in both painter and poet that this wilderness is responsible for the spiritual awakening.

The man's fashionable clothes and his walking stick suggest not so much a pilgrim as a contemporary "Everyman." His very ordinariness in this extraordinary setting is much of the point of his presence here: he is intended to be us. And of course by putting our visual perspective on the same level, Friedrich reinforces this: we don't look up to the figure, we look at him: we share his elevated vision, if at one step removed. That is, what we look at primarily is the bold, jagged rock and the man perched on top; what the man looks at is mist—the abyss.

The foreground of the painting is almost entirely eliminated, which intensifies the sojourner's isolation and exposure. But the predominant mood of the painting is not terror. This is a man, one senses, who gives himself freely to the infinite before him. It is this openness to wilderness, in fact, which seems to make possible the confident faith represented by the man's position on this exposed rock. His stance—one foot forward, close to the edge, but balanced—conveys no sense of desperation or madness. This is not Byron's Manfred about to hurl himself over the cliffs; it is Wordsworth's "human Wanderer," who beholds in the rising sun and mist "the emblem of a mind / That feeds upon infinity, that broods / Over the dark abyss. . . ."[2] Poised, confidant, moving forward to the very edge of understanding, all he can do now is to give himself over to the view—to the fog, the mountains, the steep cliffs. He has risen up out of the dark rock into the light of the blue and white sky (the Madonna's colors). In doing so there is both a sense of power in the human achievement (the literal elevation one gains in ascending the mountain suggests a simultaneous spiritual heightening, conveyed both by the stance and the point of view, which refuses to diminish the pilgrim) and also a recognition of limits. On the cliff's edge the seer—like the contemplative—is firmly anchored on solid rock and elevated into the heavens.

Caspar David Friedrich: Wanderer above the Mists

If in a traditional western religious painting we might expect to see saints standing or kneeling by the Madonna in a generic landscape, often in Friedrich (a confirmed, lifelong Protestant) the Madonna is replaced by wilderness, which doesn't simply mediate but itself embodies the divine. Here the individual gazes out into the blue the way a Catholic might gaze up at the ascension of Mary—or a traditional Protestant would gaze into the Bible. In turn, if traditionally Jesus or Mary was the mediator between God and mankind, it now becomes the role of art to become (in Friedrich's words) the "mediator between nature and mankind."

This helps locate much of the power of these paintings, and by implication Friedrich's understanding of the function of art: if wilderness is inherently divine, and leads one to union, then so too might art, which puts us at the same sublime level (if once removed). We too ascend—through contemplation of the painting itself, which intends to awaken the same elevated thoughts and feelings as the landscape. Friedrich wrote: "Just as the pious man prays without speaking a word and the Almighty hearkens unto him, so the artist with true feelings paints and the sensitive man understands and recognizes it."

This is another way of acknowledging the radically non-narrative (or non-allegorical) nature of Friedrich's landscapes. While Friedrich was once convinced to give a program guide to a painting *(The Cross In the Mountains),* his explanation no more explains the painting than Coleridge's marginal comments on "The Rime of the Ancient Mariner" explain what the Mariner sees. Such works both seek and transcend analysis. Like the parables of Jesus, or Zen koans, and like the wilderness itself, they open us to what lies on the other side of explanation.

Art, Friedrich wrote, is "the language of our feeling, our disposition, indeed, even our devotion and our prayers." Yet, as William Vaughan adds, "Friedrich was in no doubt that these feelings, whatever their origins, were religious ones . . . [his] pictures are less statements than meditations on death and salvation."[3]

It was left to Rothko and others to eliminate the human entirely from this wilderness scene, so that we ourselves might stand exactly where this man—and the individual in Friedrich's *Monk by the Sea*—stand, with nothing between us and a direct experience of the unnameable. Yet one feels already the powerful link between wilderness, art and spirit in Friedrich's work; and seeing it here in a wilderness landscape helps us to see it when we come to the abstractions of Rothko, Newman, Pollock and Still. Here too, we feel, is a kind of wilderness, a mirror for the infinite expanse of inner space. In gazing at these paintings we are not seeking solutions to a mystery; we are on the verge of becoming the mystery ourselves.

Caspar David Friedrich: Wanderer above the Mists

NOTES

1 Hugh Honour, *Romanticism* (New York: Harper & Row, 1979), pp.28–29.

2 Wordsworth's Prelude. Book 14, lines 70–3.

3 William Vaughan, *German Romantic Painting* (New Haven: Yale University Press, 1980), p. 74.

CHAPTER TWO

Of Rivers and Religion

> *If reader, I had ampler space in which*
> *to write I'd sing—though incompletely—*
> *that sweet draft for which my thirst was limitless . . .*
> —Dante[1]

1

Cold water in the mountains. Kneeling on the wet rocks in the early evening dusk beside Rainbow Creek as it rolls down from Macalester Pass, lichen and moss covering the stones, the footing delicate. Through crevices thousands of feet above, through fog and snow, it all drops into my hands. I wash the tin plates slowly.

My twelve-year-old daughter is here, drying the dishes, waiting for me to continue the tale we tell as we travel through the mountains.

The story tonight is the sound of falling water. Inside that sound is a stone, a well, an old and unforgiving man.

Unforgiven? Katie asks.

Close enough.

He lives alone. He draws his water and carries it in a wooden bucket and pours it into an old steam kettle, which he places on the darkened metal of the stove. As he sits he waits, reading by the light of the fire lines of *terza rima* so familiar he could sing them in his sleep. He lays the book in his lap every few minutes and listens to the wind, to the rain against the roof and windows. He knows the Princess is lost on the mountain and will soon be lead to his door. It is for this that he is prepared. He has waited for years; he has sung her down to him like the moon. He knows he is to be her teacher, and she his final, his best-loved student. His daughter.

I lay my hands in the water. Wind soughs through the pines. Poetry, I'm thinking; this earth is a single vowel.

Go on, Katie says.

I start again as I finish the last of the pans, placing the tiny bottle of Dr. Bonner's biodegradable soap in its small plastic bag. I say *He sings down the moon for her.*

What?

He sings down the moon. I mean he has waited for her his whole life, and his waiting is about to end. He sits in his tiny cabin and listens to the rain pour down, and he wants only to save her from this loneliness he feels.

He feels?

She feels I mean. This terrible fear of the storm. But he knows he cannot. No more could you aid a butterfly as it frees itself of the cocoon.

Couldn't you just cut a little with a pair of scissors? Gently pull out the wings?

No. It can't be done. The creature will never have the strength to fly. And so he must sit and wait.

How does he know she's coming?

Ah, he knows all right. He's studied the way things are. He can sense things shift in the air, he smells them in the wind like a bird, feels the currents like a fish.

And what has happened to the old man's wife?

Well, I begin, and pause, for I realize that I do not know. *He lost her,* I say, *a long time before.*

She died?

No. She left, or he left; he's no longer sure which, or whether perhaps it was both. Something happened between them—and ever since a door in his soul has been closed, like an unburied seed.

What do you mean?

I mean—what did I mean? *I mean that a way down to healing has shut.*

Ah, says Katie. You mean he can't love anyone.

Yes. I suppose that's what I mean.

And? She asks.

But we're finished at the creek. I stand, putting a hand out, and we walk together back up the path, carrying the dishes to the campsite where Judy has finished setting up the tent. It's approaching dark under the trees and we stumble about, laughing and crashing into one another, wet and dirty and tired. Down below I can hear it, that rushing water, and I know just where it's going, pulled headlong by its own desire. It's released from before and after. It's free inside of gravity.

2

you are a fountain in the garden
a well of living waters
that stream from Lebanon
   —Song of Solomon

It's a story of rivers, living water. Vowels and consonants riffing over stones and sediment, over the tongue and teeth of the breathing land. It's beautifully liquid all the way down.

That night, after Katie dropped off to sleep in the tent, I picked up *Siddhartha* for the first time in decades. *How he loved this river,* I read, *how it enchanted him, how grateful he was to it! In his heart he heard the newly awakened voice speak, and it said to him, "Love this river, stay by it, learn from it."*

It is, I suspected, the idea of a river that Hesse has in mind here, and not any river in particular. But this would not have occurred to me when I first read this, at the age of sixteen, when I myself did not really know any rivers except the Desplaines as it ran through Thatcher Woods, just west of Chicago. I did not think of the Desplaines when I read these words. At sixteen, love itself was little more than a sound to me, a mere hum in the heart. I had no idea what it took out of you.

But I adored Siddhartha, and understood his restlessness, his longing for the pure drone of moving waters. Even more I understood his old friend Govinda, who finds, late in his life, the enlightened Siddhartha working as a simple ferryman. *Tell me one word,* Govinda pleads, *tell me something I can conceive, something I can understand! My path,* he says, *is often hard and dark.*

Siddhartha invites his friend to kiss him on the forehead. As he does, Govinda experiences *samadhi,* a moment of pure bliss. He sees not Siddhartha's face, but others, many, a *long series, a continuous stream of faces.* He sees the face of a fish, a carp, a newborn child. He sees the face of a murderer, "saw him plunge a knife into the body of a man." It's all there in the face of Siddhartha, all choices in this or some other lifetime. It's this Govinda kissed: this reality of life flowing through one single point, *bindu,* the soundless point out of which all sound flows, the hidden peak from which all waters run.²

I remember finishing this book for the first time lying in my bedroom one warm August evening—posters of Jim Morrison and Dylan on the walls, the cover of Van Morrison's *Astral Weeks* propped up beside the small record player on the desk—and then walking outside into the night. I lay on the hill across the playground from my old school and stared up through the limbs of the elms into the dark sky. There was, I knew, nothing to be done. And I would, I knew, lose this moment, even as I knew that it had changed me, entered me in some way that I couldn't explain. I was sixteen and felt lucky, utterly graced. I'd kissed the third eye. I'd plunged into healing waters.

When I returned to *Siddhartha* we were hiking in the North Cascades from Holden, reaching Lyman Lake late in the evening. We spent two nights there before heading north over Cloudy Pass and down Agnes Gorge to Stehekin, adding a day hike up to Lyman Glacier. Between those two days I began and finished the novel again, sitting outside the tent while the light held, and then moving in and reading by flashlight while Judy read and Katie slept beside her. The lake was close, just below us, close enough to catch the sound of the headwaters as they started their long slide down to Lake Chelan.

I thought again about my own story as I lay there in the dark, my flashlight off, listening to the night whirling around me. I'd first thought of this old man as some kind of holy hermit, steeped like tea in mystical knowledge. That's what I wanted for him, but that's not how he was— at least not yet, or not entirely. *That old man needed salvation,* I realized suddenly. *He still needed those healing waters, after all those years in the mountains. They'd carried him as far as they could, cleaned him down to a kind of truth. But deeper waters awaited him.*

There are many ways of knowing a river.

Imagine making love as a river loves—the earth it wears away. That incessant and beautiful grinding, the touch of liquid against flesh, on lime and sandstone, water pulsing against the banks—this flowing of bodies together. Step off the shore into the life of another form. Discover buoyancy. Hold each other, bone and psyche worn soft by long years of bumping up against the edges. Love *is* the wearing away, like glaciers melting in the sun, a solid river of ice afloat in the sea, adrift and drawn down, evaporating by the sheer force of desire.

We have been, I thought, a channel slipping down the mountains, carving its long way home.

Under the snows and along the banks where wildflowers bloom—larkspur and lupine, gentian and bluebells, scarlet gilea and paintbrush.

Bears shuffle and deer wade, drinking of our body. Elk and antelope, deer and marmot, Ponderosa and Douglas fir. All of us on the move.

3

In *The Gates of Light,* a thirteenth century masterpiece of Kabbalah, Rabbi Joseph Gikatilla argues that aspects of God emanate from an intertwined hierarchy of ten Spheres, the *Sephirah,* connected by channels which may be disrupted or repaired through human activity. The task of the Jew is to repair this world so that it becomes a receptacle for the heavenly Spheres' *Shefa*—its "everflow." This repair, achieved through contemplation, prayer and the fulfillment of the Torah's commandments, is a form of blessing, *Brachah,* a word that is considered synonymous with the word that shares its root, *Braichah,* pool, a receptacle for water.[3]

My daughter's seventh grade class has been exploring our neighborhood, mapping all the channels that feed Piper's Creek, which itself flows down into the salt waters of Puget Sound. Through front and backyards, often just a few feet from the houses, the kids find the pools and springs, the veins that merge downhill within the creek. They photograph, keep records and maps, and wherever possible clean out anything that's blocking the descent.

Brachah, I'm thinking, *vessel for the everflow.*
The truth. It will set you free.

So the old man leaves the mountains.
But where does he go?
I don't know. What do you think?
I think—I think he goes looking for what he's lost. And I think he goes into the city.
Why the city?

I don't know. What do you think?

Ice melts, I think, *the rivers rise and flood, carrying away so much of our lives.* But I do not say it.

I'm suddenly frightened, and it's not that I no longer know where the old man is heading. We're entering uncharted territory, which in this case isn't a mountain, but the desert of the heart. Rage and forgiveness. A death that enters singing.

4

Story itself is a kind of water, beginning as a simple stream of sound waves condensed by the canal of the ear and carried to the tight eardrum, which then vibrates. Sound knocks at the door of the middle ear. There the ossicles form a moveable bridge: the hammer picks up sound vibrations and conducts them to the inner ear through the anvil and stirrup. The sound waves are amplified and transformed into mechanical energy and then into hydraulic pressure waves within the fluid-filled inner ear, the "bony labyrinth," where hearing takes place.

Consider a story of water told to the Anthropologist Keith Basso, working among the Apaches in the American Southwest. In learning the names of places Basso is learning their stories, the connections between place and people coded like DNA into these sounds. Charles, one of his teachers, is speaking:

> Now these rocks are lying alone. No one comes to them anymore. Once this wasn't so. Long ago, people came here often. They squatted on these rocks when they filled their containers with water. They knelt on these rocks when they drank water from their hands. Our people were very grateful for this spring. It made them happy to know they could rely on it anytime. They were *glad* this place was here.
>
> Now they are coming to get water! They have been working—maybe they were digging up agave—and now they are thirsty. A man is walking in the lead with women and children behind him. The women are carrying their containers. Some have water jugs on their backs. No one is talking. Maybe there are snakes here, lying on these rocks. Yes! Now the man in

front can see them! There are snakes lying stretched out on these rocks. They are the ones who own this spring, the ones who protect it . . .

Now that man has come here. He is talking to those who protect Snakes' Water, using words they understand and doing things correctly. Soon they move off the rocks. They keep going, unalarmed, until they are out of sight. Now that man is sprinkling something on the water. It is a gift to the ones who own it. He is giving thanks to them and Water, informing them that he and the people are grateful. 'This is good,' he is saying to them. 'This is good.'

Something happens inside the word as it moves inside the listener, and something happens inside the listener, who is touched. "The three of us turn from the barren spring," Keith Basso concludes, "and together walk slowly away, lost in thought and the deepness of time, sojourners still in a distant world . . ."

The story speaks of water. But it is not just a story about water, or about the people's dependency upon water, or even about the idea of water as a living, sacred entity—water *personified* as we might say. The story is not simply *about*. It conjures. The telling—even the simple naming of the place—re-members a community.

It's like a marriage, where a single re-calling of a shared place can be enough to awaken the covenant.

The word weaves its spell within us as we consume and digest it. It's the seed, and we're (however briefly) the flower. It speaks a truth, bringing it before us again, not simply as a past event but *still, now.*

This is why Charles is so infuriated with Basso when he fails to get the word right. It's not a matter of linguistics but of respect to a living entity:

What he's doing isn't right. It isn't good. He seems to be in a hurry. Why is he in a hurry? It's disrespectful. Our ancestors made this name. They made it just as it is. They made it for a reason. *They spoke it first, a long lime ago!* He's repeating the speech of our ancestors. He doesn't know that.

They try again, this time Basso's friend shouting out "GOSHTLISH TÚ BIL SIKĄ́NÉ!" And at last "the tide has turned. Instantly the form of the name and its meaning assume coherent shape, and I know that at last I've got it: GOSHTLISH TÚ BIL SIKĄ́NÉ, or Water Lies With Mud In An Open Container." This turn is *conversion* in the truest sense.

He feels the rightness of the word in the mouth, knows its meaning in and as his own body. It is a moment of belonging, knowing that in speaking the name we come into ownership.[4]

But it is we that are owned, not the other way around.

5

In this water we are buried with Christ.
By it we share his resurrection.
Through it we are reborn by the Spirit.
—Book of Common Prayer

The old man had thought she had come to him to be taught to drink of his knowledge, but he had been wrong.

So did she go off with him when he left?
I think she did. But first they went through something there.
What do you mean?
I mean she learns from the old man that she isn't his daughter.
She isn't?
No. She's the true daughter of his wife, but born of an enchantment and long kept secret.
An enchantment? You mean some kind of romance?
Something like that. She was very young, and beautiful, and fell under the spell of a wealthy man from a distant country who promised marriage. She never saw him again.
Is this what ended the marriage? The old hermit learned the truth and couldn't forgive his wife?
Perhaps. I suppose.
So was it something else? What couldn't he forgive?
I don't know how to explain. It may not have been any one thing. It may have been—simply life.
I don't get it.
Well—
Her hair falls around her, he thinks, like falling water.
What?

She's so beautiful, his wife, and so young, and he feels so old, although he isn't. He knows somehow that they are at each other's mercy. And this terrifies him. And yet he can't speak of it.

He's afraid of her?

Yes. In a way, he is. Or he's afraid of himself. He's very gifted with his hands and is highly praised as a master craftsman, but still there's something in him that feels like stone. And she knows it, and he knows she knows it.

And he can't talk about it?

No. It's impossible. The stone gets in the way. And the worst torment, far worse than being around all those who don't know, is being around the one who knows but feels powerless to change it. And so he blamed her. He cursed her kindness, and her silence which she took for kindness.

And so he left?

Yes. And he left the small girl behind, who in spite of himself he'd grown to love. And inside his silence he waited for her.

The old man leaves the mountains.

Back from the mountains I sit at Diva, a North Seattle coffeehouse, staring at this sentence, hearing it play in the labyrinth of my brain. It is, I realize, not simply the idea of the sentence but the very sounds that entice me. It's the long *o* in *old*, and above all the rhythmic alliteration of the *m* and *n*: *man, mountain*. It's sound that unites them in their difference.

Our task, I'm thinking, is to name this world, to *speak* it in sound-symbols, thereby bringing it into a new relation with the human. It's a startling possibility, suggesting both division, a kind of fall from immediacy, and yet a new possibility of conscious relationship.

Consider the alphabet: *Alef*, the shape of this letter we call *A*, says David Abram in *The Spell of the Sensuous*, "was that of an ox's head with horns." Only later, with the Greeks, did this *Alef-Beit* become divorced from representation, so that the Greek *Alpha* is a sign for nothing more than the letter A itself. The ox, and the world with it, vanished.[5]

You can see for yourself, Charles says to Keith Basso. *It looks like its name.*

In Hebrew only the consonants are written out, suggesting that for the language to be living it needed the actual animating breath of the human voice to create the vowel. It needed *ruach*, the spirit that quickens. The act of reading, then, is a constant process of new creation. So too, traditionally, in Christian monasteries, which took over from Judaism the practice of oral reading. For the monastic reader, Ivan Illich suggests, reading is much more a "carnal activity: the reader understands the lines by moving to their beat, remembers them by recapturing their rhythm, and thinks of them in terms of putting them into his mouth and chewing. No wonder," he concludes, "that pre-university monasteries are described to us in various sources as the dwelling places of mumblers and munchers."[6]

Back home I return to my shallow explorations in Hebrew, turning this time directly to *Mem,* the letter (according to the Kabbalah) for water. I speak it aloud as I read, chanting and then meditating with its sounds: *Amah. Om. Amen.*

> *Mem* . . . the fountain of the Divine Wisdom of Torah.
> Just as the waters of a physical fountain (spring) ascend from their unknown subterranean source (the secret of the abyss in the account of Creation) to reveal themselves on earth, so does the fountain of wisdom express the power of flow from the superconscious source. In the terminology of Kabbalah, this flow is from *keter* (crown) to *chochmah* (wisdom). The stream is symbolized in Proverbs as . . . "the flowing *stream*, the source of wisdom."[7]

Think of rivers, of the body itself as a current, a series of streams circulating to the heart's sea and out again, the endless spin of water and blood. Listening to the chant of Sheila Chandra, to rain becoming a steady current flowing down the storm drains and out to the Sound, I hear again the drone of *mem* within the womb of the world.

I continue to read late into the night, the dog at my feet, Judy and Kate asleep upstairs, all of these pieces of poems and stories left for years as invisible bits in various computers, inside folders in the filing cabinet beside my desk. Unfinished business. So too with my old man, who's forever on his journey home, all he owns on his back, re-tracing his past, seeking out some truth he'd buried years before. He must, I see, remember it all. He must walk through it before it will leave him be.

His wife, I wondered; what had become of her? And this girl who'd come to him—who *was* her father? And what, I suddenly wondered, of the old man's own family?

Perhaps, Katie had said, he'd been orphaned.

Perhaps so. Perhaps his early life had been one long wandering, working mostly along the coasts, on boats, until one day he'd sailed far north—to Norway perhaps—and there stumbled upon the story of his origins in some obscure mountain village.

And that's where he met his wife.

Yes. His beauty, his dark haired joy.

Dark? In Norway?

Well, that was part of her mystery of course—where she really came from.

Of course. But where did she come from?

It's bedtime.

It was, I was thinking, later that night, *the mountain and the river that they had shared, and that they had lost. Perhaps she was herself the child of the mountain, of living waters. She had all the graces of the earth and sea—and in his anger he'd fled. He'd gone one way, ascending, trying to leave everything of earth behind. But of course he carried it all with him.*

In Dante the spiraling descent of the Inferno is itself an inverted mountain, a perfect mirror of Mount Purgatory: one necessitates the other; one *creates* the other. With the fall of Satan a new kind of consciousness enters into the world. It is both the end of something and a new beginning: being stuck inside of this egotistic perspective is hell, but if *moved through,* this knowledge becomes the place from which we finally and appropriately leap off the earth entirely, carrying her within us.

The snake, perhaps, wasn't lying when he said to Eve that she will come to know as God knows. Neither, however, did he inform her what the journey would cost.

Purgatory, where my old man finds himself, is not simply a place; it's the *act* of seeing one's truth clearly. It ends in fire, and only then yields back to water. Flowing down the mountain, the healing river of Lethe reaches the base and descends below the earth, following the track carved out by the plummeting Satan, reaching at last the great refusal of reality in the frozen pool of Cocytus. This is ground zero, where nothing true is recalled, where forgetting is not blessing but evasion.

Carried on Virgil's back, Dante is literally turned around on the great body of Satan, who becomes in this way—in his own despite—the vessel of ascent. *Brachah.*

Virgil and Dante climb out of Hell together, a father and a son, finding their way by moving *against* the flow of this stream inside the darkened body of the earth. The climb, then, is not one of forgetting (such is Lethe's meaning) but its reversal, *remembering*. This stream Dante calls Eunoe, a word coined from two Greek roots, *eu* plus *nous*: good mind or memory. But the source of these two streams is the same, issuing "from a pure and changeless fountain."

> On this side it descends with power to end
> one's memory of sin; and on the other,
> it can restore recall of each good deed.
> To one side, it is Lethe, on the other,
> Eunoe; neither stream is efficacious
> unless the other's waters have been tasted:
> their savor is above all other sweetness. (*Purgatorio* 28)

In Dante what we forget are the wounds of a lifetime, represented on the climb up Purgatory by the seven p's carved onto the forehead of every pilgrim: p as in *peccatum,* sin, our attachments and addictions. As we climb, moving more deeply into the truth, the load grows curiously lighter even as the way grows steeper. There is pain, but the pain now has meaning; it has *direction*. We are pulled and lifted by reality, the deepest gravity of all.

This arrival at the summit, and at the headwaters of Lethe, then, is not simply a return to the womb, to unconsciousness; Eunoe suggests instead the arrival of the Messiah, here in the form of Beatrice, representing the awakening of that good mind in each of us: we remember suddenly who we most deeply are.

We're *pure and prepared,* Dante concludes, *to climb to the stars.*

6

It has grown late. I sit here looking out at the darkened world with a paperback Dante in my lap, a book that cost me the price of a double tall mocha, mass produced, machine-inked with words in Italian first set down from the hand of a Florentine living in exile almost 700 years ago, struggling to write his way free of bitterness and rage. In Seattle the flooding from the rains knocks houses from their foundations, closes bridges and highways. Traffic, like debris, gets stuck or finds another way around. The Lincoln bedroom. A billion dollar sale of Boeing 757s to China, nurtured, perhaps, by campaign contributions, all trickling down to—well, to me, sitting here at home, comfortably employed in a booming Northwest economy.

The eternal and the temporary fires, Virgil tells Dante; you've seen them both.

Worlds turn around me as I sit, breathing in these beautiful sounds, holding this book in my lap. Through fire and water, the desert of the heart, the end of all known roads. *Io ritornai da la santissima onda / rifattto sì come piante novelle / rinovellate di novella fronda.* I returned, says Dante, from those holy waters remade, as new plants are renewed with new leaves.[8]

"You are all beautiful, my beloved one, there is no blemish in you." So sings Host to Guest in the Song of Songs. Thus, writes Rabbi Ginsburgh, "the innate love of G-d present in every Jewish soul is compared to water. In the prayer for rain . . . we ask G-d to 'remember the father (Abraham) who was drawn after you like water.' Loving G-d, as natural to every Jewish soul as downstream flow is to water, is our inheritance from our first father Abraham."[9]

So does Beatrice tell Dante as they soar into Paradise, lifted off the surface of the earth through sheer desire for God:

> You should—if I am right—
> not feel more marvel at your climbing than
> you would were you considering a stream
> that from a mountain's height falls to its base. *(Paradiso 1)*

We flow as we are called. Gravity is particular to a situation: a small body on the surface of the earth is pulled by the weight of the earth, which seems then to be its home, until with increasing consciousness we widen our perspective and discover that the entire earth feels the pull of a greater force yet—and so on beyond the solar system and out to the edges of the universe.

Gravity in Dante is another name for desire (*de-sidus,* from the star): what pulls everything is "the love that turns the sun and other stars." Water flows, as the poet Li Po says; the peach trees blossom.

Memories too. Stories of places shared with family and friends flow into story, into poetry, into names. That old man and the child from my story, for instance, who make their way together down the valley, seeking the mother, the wife—seeking the future in an unfinished past.

But what happens then? Katie asks; it's bedtime, at home, as we finish the story.

Well, I say, *they were free. They knew where they were going, even if they didn't know where they were going.*

I get it.

Good.

Is this where you quote from Milton?

What makes you ask that?

Because you always quote from Milton.

Do I?

You do.

Well, I guess this is the time. So—

I know. "Hand in hand, with wandering steps and slow, they took their solitary way."

What's that from?

I don't know.

Paradise Lost.

Right. Adam and Eve. Booted from the Garden by God's angel. Flaming swords—I remember that bit.

In Milton it's quite moving, actually, especially at the end. It's both devastating and yet—it's like the beginning of a whole new adventure. Which it is. Which we are.

I turn out the light, say the magic words, assuring us both that everything's safe and secure, and then I linger a moment more, wanting and yet never quite wanting to go. Finally I wander into my own shared bedroom, where I slip beneath the sheet and back into another story.

Re-membering: heading into the mountains along the winding Skagit River, Judy behind the wheel in the pre-dawn dark, Katie asleep beside her, and myself in the back, meditating, moving in and out of worlds, the land flowing by like a great brown river. Realizing, as I slipped lightly out, how bound I am by my own consciousness, and by this earth. And yet how easy it is to float like a dancer, to move so delicately inside these sounds, borne inside the world's great body.

Of Rivers and Religion

NOTES

1 The title is in homage to guitarist John Fahey and his 1972 Warner Bros. LP *Of Rivers and Religion*. The epigraph is from Dante's *Purgatorio,* canto 33, translated by Allan Mandelbaum (Bantam, 1986). All subsequent quotations from *Purgatorio* and *Paradiso* are from Mandelbaum except where noted below.

2 Herman Hesse, *Siddhartha* (New York: New Directions, 1951) pp. 82–83, 120–2.

3 *Gates of Light (Sha 'are Orah)* is translated by Avi Weinstein (Harper Collins, 1994. See especially pp. xviii–xi, 16, 19–21, 24, 37.

4 Keith Basso, *Wisdom Sits in Places* (University of New Mexico Press, 1996), p. 10–11, 15.

5 The *alef,* the first letter in the Hebrew alphabet, is formed by drawing two *yuds,* one to the upper right and the other to the lower left, joined by a diagonal *vav.* See Rabbi Yitzchak Ginsburgh, *The Alef-Beit* (Aronson, 1995), p. 24. See also David Abram's *The Spell of the Sensuous* (Pantheon 1996), p. 101.

6 Ivan Illich, *In The Vineyard of the Text* (University of Chicago, 1995), p. 54.

7 *Alef-Beit*, p. 194.

8 Dante, *Purgatorio* 33, my translation.

9 *Alef-Beit*, p. 200.

Interlude

Crossing the Threshold

Some hours later they were liberated by the American Army near the town of Dachau. The American commander forced the local townspeople to come and see what the glorious Third Reich had done to humanity. An elderly women . . . stared at Livia with great compassion. Finally she said to her, "It must have been very difficult for people your age to endure all this suffering."
"How old do you think I am?" Livia asked her.
"Maybe sixty, maybe sixty-two," replied the German women.
"Fourteen," replied Livia.
The German women crossed herself in horror and fled.
—Hasidic Tales of the Holocaust

The Stranger may not be so far away: behind a prison wall, or simply across the street. This elderly woman, for instance, merely has to step outside and see what she had for so long refused to admit. Even then her expression changes to horror as she looks more deeply into this young woman's face; the truth she sees she cannot endure.

It can happen this suddenly; a chance meeting, the death of a loved one, a child, and suddenly the familiar turns to strange. My grandfather seemed so at home in his tiny Chicago apartment with his books and his Sibelius, but after my grandmother died he attempted suicide, suddenly feeling bereft. The familiar had suddenly become foreign to him, and death seemed less strange than simply going on.

We learn to flee the stranger, the unfamiliar face on the dark street, even though so much learning comes from precisely those times when we have crossed some border and entered into the unknown—a lesson we begin to learn as soon as we emerge from the womb.

A friend of mine spends his days on the streets of Seattle working with such strangers: in his case the mentally ill homeless. He does not preach to them, nor does he provide money. When asked for a handout he suggests places to find shelter or a meal. Above all he listens. He stays on the street and offers his mind and heart. He invites them in, one by one.

Success is slow, if indeed the word is meaningful at all. The folks Craig works with tend to vanish, unaccountably disappearing from one day or one hour to the next. A vision or a voice seizes them and they're gone, off to California or Canada. But Craig's back again the next day, not expecting to cure the world, and indeed not expecting anything at all. He lopes along, at ease on the streets because he has nothing to lose or protect. He's at home there in the unbounded, where nothing at all is foreign.

"It's a question of story," Craig tells me as we stroll along one day. "That's how anyone becomes familiar to us. This old woman for instance, Marie, who camped out down near Pike Place Market. A wild woman, totally shocking. Electric. And yet she also seemed defenseless, as if lost—so lost that she wasn't even aware how strange she appeared to others."

He paused, thinking. "Remember that character in 'Kubla Khan'? 'And all should cry, Beware! Beware! / His flashing eyes, his floating hair!' That was Marie.

"The first day I see her I walk up to her, introduce myself, we talk and I move off. I see her again, the next and the next. Little by little I hear pieces of a story—usually fantastic (and sometimes fantasized) and often truly horrible.

"But I keep listening—I've got no other agenda." Craig laughs.

"It helps," he continues, "that I've been doing this for a while, and have some psychological training. It allows me a bit of comfort. But that can hinder as much as help. A lot of my job involves my willingness to visit her on her own territory—and to learn from her. I have to cross over the threshold and share something of what she sees."

"Cross her threshold?"

"Yes. I can't pigeonhole her from a safe distance. I can't make assumptions without knowing her. It's too easy to put a psychological frame around her: she's manic-depressive; she's schizophrenic, whatever. These words stop the exchange between us. It's odd, because they seem to make these strangers more familiar, the way any label does. But they're deceptive: a partial truth at best, like labeling someone WASP, Jew, Indian, lawyer, insurance salesman. Marie may be manic-depressive—and she may be an insurance salesman for all I know—but these facts tell me little. The real point is simply for me to be on her side, no questions asked. That's what I mean by crossing the threshold."

"That's hard work—and frightening."

"Sure. Sometimes it is. People have hard lives. But illnesses are usually there for a reason—the mental disturbance is itself a kind of boundary. It seems to protect the defenseless, like a kind of mask. It also conveys a certain power, and so many people tend to fear it. It can be difficult being around someone like Marie. She doesn't seem to make sense, she may grab you to make a point—she doesn't observe the normal, invisible lines that separate us, whether those lines are linguistic or physical. And so yes: frightening. These are definitely strange people, but beautiful."

I looked at Craig. "Beautiful?"

He laughed at my expression. "Absolutely. Often very tender, and incredibly courageous. Heroic. They do us all a great service."

"How so?"

"They keep us honest. Sometimes they truly do see something that most of us miss. If nothing else they make us face what we'd rather not face. Above all, our fear."

We walked on in silence, and I watched as Craig moved about the park, greeting some haggard-looking men as old friends, introducing himself to others. And then we moved on.

"It helps, of course," he continued, still thinking about Marie, "that I'm not a doc, not a nurse, not a cop, and not a social worker. I'm not trying to get anything from her. Instead I'm simply a reminder, a visitor from an old place that she has left and lost.

"Eventually I accompanied Marie to the hospital, and watched from day to day as she slowly came back to herself. I listened as she told me how she'd suffered from recurrent periods of depression and disorientation. Her memory goes; she ceases to recognize friends and family. There are moments of ecstasy, but others of real hell. And then she said something striking—absolutely lucent: 'when I'm out there there's never any guide.'"

Craig and I stopped for a cup of coffee. "I told her about possible medications," he said to me, "but I also mentioned the Sibyl, the one who informs Aeneas of the way through Hades. It was clear that—like most of us—she couldn't possibly be expected to negotiate that underworld on her own: We are strangers there. But—I said to her—if you had a guide, a sibyl—what then?"

"And?" I asked.

"Well," Craig leaned back, "of course the idea pleased her immensely. She was enchanted—as who wouldn't be? 'A sibyl' she said, over and over; 'how lovely!'"

The Sibyl. The prophetess, one who speaks truth, but in a kind of fury, under the fierce inspiration of a god. "Weave a circle 'round her thrice," Coleridge might well warn. So too in Virgil:

> Her face and color alter suddenly; her hair
> is disarrayed; her breast heaves, and her wild
> heart swells with frenzy . . .

And this is supposed to be Aeneas' guide.

Just who is the strange one here? The answer is not so simple. It may best be defined as whoever it is that crosses the threshold. The Sibyl herself is taken over by the god and so becomes a visionary, unknown even to herself. But the stranger here is also the sane Aeneas, who lost himself in losing a home and family in Troy. Despite appearances, he is the one in need of a guide.

"Easy," the Sibyl warns,

> the way that leads into Avernus: day
> and night the door of darkest Dis is open.
> But to recall your steps, to rise again
> into the upper air: that is labor.[1]

This, I suddenly realized, was Craig's point: he works with people who have lost the way back, who have needed a guide in order to get out—and who are themselves potential healers, sibyls themselves.

The simplest thing to say about Craig's work is that he is there in service to these lost souls, but I suspect that this is not the entire story. They may need a few of us as guides, but so too, it seems, do we need them. We see something in their presence, something uncanny, *unheimlich* (as Freud might say): something unhomelike. They carry us into the unknown.

So too, surely, did people feel about St. Francis—not to mention Jesus.

Welcome the stranger, we are told in so many tales; I think of the wandering Odysseus, of Philemon and Baucis, and of Lot. Who knows whether that stranger may be an angel or a god? But what does this mean except that this stranger is always a kind of door into a new life, a life, finally, without thresholds, without boundaries, without fear?

Like the old woman of Dachau, we may choose or not to open the door to this stranger. To take the risk, we know, may be to open ourselves to the influence of the god. An old identity may be lost, or an old way of seeing that felt safe because it closed out the Other.

NOTES

1 From *The Aeneid,* translated by Allen Mandelbaum (University of California Press, 1971), Book 6.

CHAPTER THREE

Walking among the Fires

If the Spectator could Enter into these Images in his Imagination approaching them on the Fiery Chariot of his Contemplative Thought . . . or could make a Friend & Companion of one of these Images of wonder which always entreats him to leave mortal things as he must know then would he arise from his Grave then would he meet the Lord in the Air & then he would be happy.
—Blake, *A Vision of the Last Judgment*

A Last Judgment is Necessary because Fools flourish.
—Blake, *A Vision of the Last Judgment*

1

The three of us were in Washington's Methow Valley, hiking north from Highway 20, close to viewing range of Canada, telling stories, singing and complaining about the bugs. At night after settling into camp we'd read aloud from *The Subtle Knife*, Phillip Pullman's sequel to *The Golden Compass*. It's a mysterious story, involving a spirit-like substance called Dust, the twelve year old heroes Lyra and Will, a beautiful witch named Serafina Pekkala and a knife that cuts open the space between worlds. And daemons: a conscious, articulate animal/soul attached to the human.

North America once ended directly east of us. About 100 million years ago the Okanagon subcontinent sailed into this landmass to begin a new coastline, ending where the Okanagon River flows. Even then the Methow was on the floor of the Pacific, submerged between the North American Plate and new plates sliding towards the coast. Shellfish lived in the shallow sea that covered the mountains we hike upon; fossil hunters have unearthed mollusks, ammonites and belemnites throughout the valley.

At about the time the dinosaurs disappeared from this area the Cascade subcontinent collided with North America, traveling northeast, breaking the land as it slid past into huge faults, when it was sculpted further by retreating glaciers. Kame terraces formed in the valley—a giant stairway rising up from the valley floor to the mountains, marking the pauses in the melting of the ice.

Here on the east side of the Cascades, where the Methow and the Pasayten Wilderness lie, the rain ends, drawn into the bowl created by the two mountain ranges. When the July temperature in Seattle is 75, across the mountains in Winthrop or Spokane it will be up in the 90s. Beyond the river valleys, irrigated and green with fruit trees, the land becomes bare and brown, the color of toasted almonds.

We camp the first night in the high country above Windy Pass. Broiled by the sun, food for mosquitoes and deerflies, we move on the next day to Goat Lakes—so named, we're convinced, because only the mountain goats can find it. Led by our daughter we spend an afternoon exploring the meadows, 6,000 feet above sea level, shot full of lupine at this time of year, and then climb the narrow stream through brambles and huckleberries in search of the upper lake where at last we strip and plunge into blue-green glacial water.

Back at the campsite we climb into the tent to escape the bugs, taking turns reading aloud. Another witch—the powerful Ruta Skadi—has taken off after the angels, shining like a million suns in the night sky. Dr. Mary Malone, who has made the acquaintance of Lyra and through her learned how to contact this angelic Dust, is asking questions of it. *Who are you? What are you?* Struggling to put together the pieces of the universe's puzzle, she finally wonders "did you intervene in human evolution?" and the answer comes back *yes*. And when asked why, a single word floats onto her computer screen: *vengeance*.[1]

For a moment we lie in the silence, tucked into our tent, listening to the space around this word.

Veangeance? Katie asks.

That's what it says. These are rebel angels, apparently, making this some kind of Gnostic children's tale (which I do not say). But if the Church is experimenting on children by surgically removing their daemons, trying to freeze innocence (and ignorance) by cutting off the soul, then, I say, rebel angels would be just who we'd root for.

I continue to read. Mary Malone is equally surprised by this answer, and quickly leaps to a staggering conclusion: *After the war in heaven—Satan and the Garden of Eden—but it isn't* true, *is it? Is that what you—?*

—But she's interrupted by this voice, which tells her *Find the Girl and the Boy. Waste no more time.*

And when she asks *why* is told, cryptically,

You must play the serpent.

I stop reading. The three of us listen to the last cry of daylight outside the tent. I lie on my back, on top of my sleeping bag, hands crossed over my chest, peaceful as sleeping Lazarus. Staring upwards I imagine limbs like a great menorah, golden arms stretched to the sky and lit by seven stars.

Like Mary, all we know is to follow the child. There is little enough to go on; all she has is what the voices tell her: *You have been preparing for this as long as you have lived.*

There are, we learn, these windows between worlds, gaps like those between mountains. *Moments in time*, Blake called them, *that Satan cannot find.*

I lie against the ground, my eyes closed, feeling the rise and fall of life as if the earth were an ocean. Breath and blood. The boundaries fall away.

2

> *Fire over water:*
> *The image of the condition before transition.*
> *Thus the superior man is careful in the differentiation of things,*
> *so that each finds its place.*
> —I Ching, *Hexagram 64,*
> *Wei Chi, Before Completion*

Instead of sleeping that night I found myself thinking about daemons, about Mary Malone, and about myself, in part because on the door of Mary Malone's office is a symbol from the *I Ching—The Book of Changes*—a text which has fascinated me since I was a teenager. In the summer of 1969, shortly after I turned sixteen, I put down six hard-earned dollars to buy myself the beautiful hardbound edition of the famous Wilhelm/Baynes translation, with Carl Jung's foreword connecting the *I Ching* to his own theories of synchronicity. As I recall it now, the timing of this purchase was no coincidence; I bought it as a birthday present for myself, following some kind of winding trail that lead from Alan Watts and Colin Wilson to Hesse and Jung and from there to mandalas and labyrinths, to Zen and Taoist poets. These became my guides through the mountains.

Into this mix came the *I Ching,* which was in fact designed to be a guide, although a truly cryptic one, not unlike the Sybil herself. My high school journals still include the pages where I posed a question— *should I quit the swim team? my life?*—and copied down the hexagram which supplied an "answer." *It furthers one to cross the great water.* Or: *The flying bird brings the message; it is not well to strive upward, it is well to remain below.*

This was clearly no magic eight ball; instead what I got for all my questioning was a kind of poetry—which, it turned out, was exactly the answer that I needed.

"A form of divination" is what Mary calls the *I Ching,* speaking to Lyra, who sees it as an equivalent to her own alethiometer: both, she says, are means of contacting this Dust. Dark Matter, Mary says, particles of consciousness.

I lie there in the dark of the tent, my eyes opened, thinking of Dust. Thinking of thinking, the joy of knowing that I know tree and water, earth and sky and mountain. Knowing that I know. But knowing too that this also means knowing, possibly, the end of knowing.

Ay, there's the rub.

"Anything that was associated with human thought was surrounded by Shadows," Mary Malone says; "there was a cutoff point about thirty, forty thousand years ago. Before that, no Shadows. After that, plenty. And that's about the time, apparently, that modern human beings first appeared."

"It's Dust", said Lyra authoritatively. "That's what it is."

It's Eve, is what I'm thinking—the beginning of language, of self-consciousness. All of that beauty and knife-tearing pain.

One thing I realize, lying there awake, is that I cannot explain to Katie the nature of the Church in this novel. All I can say is that it is driven by fear: a fear of consciousness, of desire, of change, all represented in the fact of puberty.

But Katie herself is thirteen; better than any explanation, I could say to her, is simply living her own way across that gulf.

I do not say this.

"Dust is something bad . . . something evil and wicked," Mrs. Coulter tells Lyra; she is Lyra's mother, the Church's most powerful ally. "At the age we call puberty, the age you're coming to very soon, darling, daemons bring all sorts of troublesome thoughts and feelings, and that's what lets Dust in. A quick little operation before that, and you're never troubled again. And your daemon stays with you, only . . . just not connected. Like a . . . like a wonderful pet, if you like."

Dust, Mrs. Coulter implies, is dirt, in the moral and metaphorical sense. *Filth*. It's exactly the understanding that one of my students described in an essay: as a child, she wrote, she loved playing in the dirt and mud. Only when she grew older did she learn, thanks be to God, that this earth is, well, *dirty*. It's what Christ cleanses us from. It is sin.

Lyra knows better, or at least knows deeper. This operation her mother describes is not salvation but emasculation. It reduces our beautiful animalness—our *anima*, the soul or breath of us—to the status of a pet. It tames something wild and true in us, something directly linked to consciousness, which is far more than mere rationality, just as the body is far more than biology. Consciousness is not intended to cut us off from our bodies; instead it invites us to know this relationship to the animal in a deeper way—something akin, I suspect, to the relationship between shaman and totem.

Lyra does not miss the import of this idea: to take the animal out of us is to take the soul—and with it our freedom. There is no antithesis and thus no possible synthesis. Mrs. Coulter's cut untangles the DNA. She ends the dance.

When Lyra is identified as a new Eve, bringing about, potentially, a new cycle of life, Mrs. Coulter's simple desire is to destroy her—"to prevent another Fall. . . ."

Which is why the angels tell Mary: *You must play the serpent.*

The next day we continue north, up and out at dawn to avoid the heat. We are two adults born in 1953, on the cusp of the ascension of Elvis, and a thirteen-year-old, born in 1984, the year of Orwell, Reagon and *Born In The USA*. Katie already fits into her mother's ancient flower-patched bell-bottoms and peasant blouses. I of course look at my daughter in these clothes and see a reflection of the woman I first met more than twenty years ago in Greece; a place, it seemed then, of unutterable light.

By now, of course, the vessels are broken.

But then breaking seems to be the point. When the vessels break light flows like rain, like blood. We ride against each other until that wall between us tears and something new rides in.

The three of us head for the pass, spiraling up switchbacks, silent under the strain of the ascent. It's a relief in a way; all of my attention goes into each step, the slow and steady rise to the ridge above us. I do not, for the moment, need to think. Bent under the weight of our packs, our heads lowered, we shuffle along, lifting our feet over rocks and boulders as small picas scurry along the trail ahead of us. Unable even to lift my head for long because of the pack, instead I watch my own legs, the muscles straining, skin shining with sweat.

We stop for the day at the edge of dusk. While Judy begins setting up the tent Katie and I pump water and search the trees for a suitable limb on which to hang the food. Together we talk about the parallel worlds in *The Subtle Knife,* where Lyra's daemon is external and Will's (who comes from our world) is apparently internal, even while these two share an Oxford that is geographically the same.

A mother and a father world, Katie says to me.

Will and Lyra's worlds?

Yes.

Maybe so, I admit. I pause a moment in my pumping, wondering about this. You think your mother and I inhabit different worlds?

Definitely. You're like water and fire.

Hm. One settles and one—

Rises. Flickers.

Heats? Lights?

She laughs. *If it makes you feel better.*

But, I suggest, maybe water and fire need each other. Maybe it's like Lyra and Will, They share similar roots after all.

Lyra and Will?

Fire and water. The word *burn,* for example. It's both a verb meaning to destroy by fire and a very old noun for spring or stream—like this one here.

A burning stream.

It's redundant. Get it?

Sure.

It boils and bubbles. *Brew* is from the same root. And *broth.*

Broil?

Probably. And *breed.*

And Breath? Breathe?

From the Old English *braeth*: odor, warm air, steam.

What else?

Well, *bratwurst. Brimstone. Brand. Ferment.*

Ferment?

As in yeast. Something bubbling up. A Latin root in this case, linked back to a common Indo-European root. *Fervor. Effervescent. Barmy.*

Meaning what?

Full of barm, I suppose—the yeast foam that rises to the top of fermenting malt liquors.

Beer, for example.

So barmy is—

Foamy. Frothy. Crazy.

Katie laughs. No comment necessary.

We head back up the path carrying water bottles and filter, both tired from the long day. Then Kate turns, unable to resist, and looks at me.

Do you ever get the feeling that what we're doing here is barmy?

The sun sets behind the peaks to the west a half hour later as I prepare the stove—a new MSR bought the day before when we discovered that the old stove wouldn't ignite (a fuel leak in the valve). I'd had it cleaned before we left Seattle but hadn't fired it up. My mistake, and, I found myself reflecting as I walked back to the car on the first day out, a grimly appropriate one. No combustion, and hence no fire, a problem duplicated in the old Toyota I drive, which has been badly misfiring all summer, and duplicated, it sometimes feels, in almost every area of my life. Even our house doesn't hold heat anymore; it's undergoing a badly needed healing from its years in the early seventies as the local drug house. So the old walls have come down, a poorly designed fireplace removed, and the foundations revealed. The whole place is opened up.

Judy pulls out the freeze-dried pasta primavera and pours two cups of filtered water into the pan as we swat mosquitoes in the last of the evening heat. I prime the new stove and light the match, watching carefully as the flames burn off from the priming cup and slowly heat up the main jets of the stove, at which point I slowly re-open the valve and let the white gas seep into the jets as the main burner ignites, burning wildly and then, magically, cutting into a sharp disciplined blue flame.

Water molecules go barmy.

The stove is a beautiful product of American technology, akin in its way to Will's subtle knife, *subtle* here suggesting keen, sharp, and ingenious: able to make fine distinctions. It also, of course, suggests sly, devious, and crafty, all characteristics of Lyra.

Both, perhaps, are kindred spirits to the sharpened blade of poetry, which is crafty in the ways of metaphor: both ingenious and subtle, working not by logic but by ana-logic: analogy. It invites a shift in vision—a crossing over. And this moment, Blake at least suggests, is a kind of Last Judgment: not some final exam imposed by a vengeful god, instead these flames are nothing but our own awareness of separation. They exist because consciousness exists. The fire *is* consciousness.

I watch the stove burn. It's the discipline of craft, of profound attention brought to bear on a tiny moment. *Just this, just this.*

The night comes on. Steam starts to rise. I eat, sitting on the ground between Judy and Kate, drinking a cup of tea as the cold mountain air seeps down the valley, the dark gathering around us. It's all ritual: light the stove, start a small fire to sit beside later in the evening; watch the dry larch burn, the intense energy held by the wood broken down, carbon freed into new forms. A little death.

I place my hands close to the light, watching it all go dark.

I remember when Judy and I moved out to the Northwest over twenty years ago, when we first camped together in these mountains, down south at Copper Creek, two years before we were married. Delighted by her steady attention to the mechanics of fire building, I sat there and watched the flames slowly catching from the careful accumulation of twigs, pine needles and cones. Supplemented by small branches, it would grow until the structure of larger logs were themselves slowly consumed, becoming at last part of what they framed.

As do we all.

Our extremes meet up here in the mountains, I first realized then; like Lyra and Will, our differences mesh. At six thousand feet much of the inessential drops away and we find ourselves rooted in each other.

I remember watching the sun drop behind the peaks that first time in the mountains, breathing the immense space of the forest, that great and living darkness. The flames from Judy's fire carved out a beautiful room: red walls, a perfect sonnet.

In the tent that night we finish Chapter Thirteen, "Aesahaettr," a title that refers to something Lord Asriel (Lyra's father) needs in order to defeat the Authority. The word sounds, Serafina Pekkala says to Ruta Skadi, like "god destroyer," and may refer to the subtle knife that Will carries, or to Lyra herself, this new Eve. But surely all this suggests that a god who can be destroyed is no real god at all but a projection, or what Blake would call a Specter, meaning something within us that, projected outward, separates us from our own truth. So too in *The Subtle Knife*, where the Specters (the novel's word, as it is Blake's) devour the adults but have no power over the pre-conscious children.

"They traveled on through the day," I read aloud by flashlight, Judy and Katie deep and comfortable beside me, "resting, moving, resting again, as the trees grew thinner and the land more rocky. Lyra checked the alethiometer: *keep going*, it said; *this is the right direction*."

They are, like the three of us, heading north, guided by Lyra's golden compass. At chapter's end, however, the two witches are startled out of their discussion about Lord Asriel's campaign by a flash where Lyra lies sleeping.

> They stood, alarmed that something had slipped past their guard, and saw a gleam of light from the camping place; not firelight though, nothing remotely like firelight. . . .
>
> All the witches were asleep on the grass, and so were Will and Lyra. But surrounding the two children were a dozen or more angels, gazing down at them.
>
> And then Serafina understood something for which the witches had no word: it was the idea of pilgrimage. She understood why these beings would wait for thousands of years and travel vast distances in order to be close to

something important, and how they would feel differently for the rest of time, having been briefly in its presence. That was how these creatures looked now, these beautiful pilgrims of rarified light, standing around the girl with the dirty face and the tartan skirt and the boy with the wounded hand who was frowning in his sleep.

'They have no flesh,' Ruta Skadi says to Serafina Pekkala, 'did you see that? All they are is light. Their senses must be so different from ours....'

These are beings of light, of fire. We're drawn to their lack of gravity, the ease of their fleshless grace. Yet so too are these ancient flames drawn to us out of their "starved Presence." They *need* us: we are the wick.

"How much they must miss," Serafina Pekkala thought, "never to feel the earth beneath their feet, or the wind in their hair, or the tingle of starlight on their bare skin!"

Bodiless souls, pure uncomplicated consciousness, these creatures come from great distances not just to pass on a message; they stand by us because they *long* to. There is something about our terrible weight they cannot resist.

3

At 5,000 feet I watch water begin to steam. Judy is already rolling up the tent while Katie struggles into her cold boots. After a quick breakfast of oatmeal and tea we again head north, walking close to fourteen miles up and down ridges to an unnamed summit just above Hopkins Lake, almost within hailing distance of the Canadian border.

All through the day, prompted by thoughts of the young heroine of this novel, and by the sight of Katie, I found myself wandering back to myself at the age of thirteen, comparing what I remembered to what I saw before me in my daughter. While I was a popular kid—an athlete, which helped—already the decency I showed to adults didn't match something dark and dangerous I felt crawling around inside me. Some daemon of my own, I suppose, trying to find its form. Some snake with a flickering tongue.

Autumn days I walked to school beneath burning maples and oaks, the air within me smoldering. I'd create long stories of a people living far below the earth's surface when all the land was locked in ice. The only fire strong enough to free us was at the center of the planet or in the stars, unknown to all but poets and singers, mages who saw the entire body of the planet shifting and roiling, rising and settling into mountain ranges, into valleys and plains. They sang rivers. They sang frog and bear, bacteria and DNA. They sang the possibility of change.

Weekend nights I'd watch TV and take long showers while listening to music on the portable phonograph I'd haul into the bathroom. Nico and Dylan, The Incredible String Band, Van Morrison.

> And he raised his hand up into the nighttime sky
> To count the stars shining in her eyes

I'd sit there and float inside the burning water, the blade of that voice pulling me out to sea.

Katie hikes along before me, her long blonde hair tied back, her strong legs climbing over the rocks, eager to get to the top of the ridge. I climb, following my daughter, then glance back at my wife who for the moment walks behind, shadowing our steps. I catch her eye, never sure what I'm going to find. All the world of not-me seems contained in her. No wonder a simple turn—a word, a look—can hold such surprise: each time it's a brand new world.

> *Figliuol mio,* Virgil says,
> *qui può esser tormento, ma non morte.*
> *Ricorditi, ricorditi!*

> My son, though there may be
> suffering here, there is no death.
> Remember! Remember!

But still, Dante writes, *I joined my hands, and stretched them out to fend the flames.*[2]

Walking among the Fires

At the end of the day's hike I lie on the ground, stretching my sore muscles. I arch my back to the sky, forming a bridge, a semicircle in the air, as if my other half were buried inside the earth.

Night comes on. I fire up the stove and the three of us sit side by side on logs as we eat, talking about blisters and counting up our bites. For a moment, before Katie and I go down to the stream to wash the dishes, we all just stare out at the darkening meadow, entranced by the slow withdrawal of light.

It's hard to move, Katie finally says.

I nod.

But it's a good kind of hard.

Yes, I say. It's like you've done it. Done enough.

We finally force ourselves to our feet and down to the stream, walking gingerly along the narrow path that leads behind the tent, through the trees and around at last to the rocks where we can sit and scrub out the cups and bowls and pan. I wash, singing *Oh weary pilgrim, welcome home.* I sing

> Clouds so swift
> Rain won't lift
> Gate won't close
> Railing's froze
> Get your mind off wintertime
> You ain't goin' nowhere.

Later when Judy and Kate go into the tent I remain outside, sitting cross-legged on the cold ground. I close my eyes. I do not move. I sit like an open door, a mole's hole.

I hear laughter inside the tent and then zippers on sleeping bags. I put my hands in my lap and sense the light of the lantern flicker and go out. I listen. More laughter. Wind. A drop of rain.

For some reason—perhaps that flickering light—I suddenly remember a scene from Tarkovsky's *Nostalgia* where a man stands astride a statue of Marcus Aurelius in Rome's Campidoglio and prophesies to a bored crowd. He pours gasoline over his head, his back, his chest. *Music!* he cries.

Freude, shöner Götterfunken,
Tochter aus Elysium,
Wir betreten feuertrunken,
Himmlische, dein Heiligtum.

The man flicks his lighter, the wind rising as his body of water marries flame.

Deine Zauber binden wieder,
Was die Mode streng geteilt;
Alle Menschen werden Brüder,
Wo dein sanfter Flügel weilt.³

His clothes ignite. The music lifts as he falls from the platform.

In the tent a flashlight turns on; Katie reads aloud from *The Subtle Knife*. When I open my eyes I see the circle of light spill over the walls. *On said the alethiometer,* Katie reads. *Farther. Higher.*

In the film a loose wire breaks the connection in the tape recorder resting on the stones of the plaza and so we watch the old man stagger and die without a soundtrack. He gasps and chokes, his back on fire. His dog Zoe, chained to the wall, howls in despair. No one else moves.

You witches know something about the child, Mrs. Coulter shouts. *Name her!*

In agony the witch cries, *Eve! Mother of all! Eve, again!*

The old man in the film continues to burn as the scene cuts to the main character, a Russian writer who is suffering from nostalgia, that ache for home. He'd made a promise to the old man so he takes the taxi to St. Catherine's Springs only to find that the healing waters have been drained away. The writer takes the gift of the old man's candle and lights it, touching the side of the pool before beginning his ritual walk to the other end.

The candle blows out.

He returns, re-lights the candle and begins again, slowly walking as the camera follows him. He covers the flame with his coat and his free hand. In a single long take the camera follows him across the pool until, a few feet from the end, the candle again goes out.

He stands there looking around, exhausted and angry. He does not know what he's doing. He does not know anything.

He sits like a frog inside his cold hole. Like an embittered seed.

But the camera is a persistent dog. She will not turn away, will not allow a single moment when we are not focused on the man's face and hands. An entire company of fools—director and crew, actors and stagehands—devotes itself to this man carrying a burning candle across an empty pool. And so now do I.

We sit in the dark of the theater following a flickering light.

The writer returns once more to the edge of the pool, lights the candle for the third time and again begins walking. As he reaches the end the engine to this rusty universe begins to turn over. A spark jumps a gap. And as I sit outside the tent seeing this all again I suddenly remember a late afternoon thirty years ago *when I sit beneath a tree with my girlfriend who would be dead in three years and we move closer, out of the rain, far beneath the heavy branches of the willow, both of us crying, our backs against the thick trunk, not speaking but turning to each other, lightly touching each other's face, the salt of each other, wanting to be inside each other, wet as otters, slick as seals.*

The writer touches the wall. He drops to the bottom of the empty pool and his candle goes out.

Ah, said Mrs. Coulter.

And she breathed a great sigh, as if the purpose of her life was clear to her at last.

A few minutes later I climb into the tent, joining my wife and daughter, looking up to the stars before I zip the door and close us all in. *The first heaven's Seven Stars,* Dante writes; *those stars that never rise or set*—the seven stars of the Little Dipper, *Ursus Minor,* which guide the navigator's eye to the North Star. Here they lead to Dante's beloved Beatrice.

> "Guardaci ben! Ben son, ben son Beatrice.
> Come degnasti d'accedere al monte?
> Non sapei tu che qui è l'uom felice?"

> "Look here! For I am Beatrice, I am!
> How were you able to ascend the mountain?
> Did you not know that man is happy here?"

Moonlight threads the eye of the needle through the mountain pass. In my dreams we're walking through that gap, singing as we go.

4

Somewhere life has taken a wrong turn. The naturalist and philosopher Paul Shepard would say that it was back in the Neolithic when we began our steady domination over the wild. Cultivation and agriculture led to surplus food and storage, which lead in turn to city walls and armies. It deepened the division between inside and outside, us and them, which language and consciousness began. And this is where we still are.

We've turned back south today, heading home. The sun as we walk is on our left, the day already heating up by ten in the morning. But whatever resistance I had to walking seems to melt away. Heat is heat, death is death. My daemon rides on my shoulder, singing as I walk the dusty trail.

> Well the first days are the hardest days
> don't you worry any more
> 'Cause when life looks like easy street
> There is danger at your door

All things break down, I'm thinking; they melt, evaporate, vaporize and die, disintegrating back to carbon and nitrogen.

No, I'm, thinking, is a room inside the house of *Yes.*

That house is a burning forest.

Inside this forest a boy lies down and buries himself beneath the October leaves. He breathes in the cold air of this beautiful world. O, *Holy One* he hears rising up from the smoke; O, *Holy One, Holy and Strong, Holy and Immortal.* He turns among the spinning worlds, around the words of *l'amor che move il sole e l'altre stelle.* He's riding inside her beautiful spine of fire.

Love, I'm thinking, is the subtlest knife.

5

Home after our ten days in the mountains I return to the work on the house and to my books, the newspaper, and movies. The sun shines and the weeds grow. It's a tomb, this beautiful world. I take out the garbage, run the dog, sand down doors and paint walls, so tired of the construction work that I'm ready to hurl paint like Jackson Pollock. Instead I go outside and stare across the mountains into a dark western sky.

It doesn't matter what I do. Wherever I turn I face a wall of flame, my own burning self.

I have coffee and dessert with Judy—it's a Saturday night in September, the mountains a distant memory—and try to explain how it is that I want to kill her. It's difficult to describe because the desire has little in fact to do with her. Like everything else she's simply in my way. She's what I bump up against, what rubs me raw. She's out there beyond my control.

Two teenagers in Seattle set a homeless man on fire, offended by capitalism's failure to answer the question of his existence. Two boys in Georgia open fire on their own grade school classmates as if it were a video game. Another in Oregon, in Texas, in Washington, in Colorado. A kid in Tennessee knifes his divorced mother and then walks to school and shoots his ex-girlfriend, her new boyfriend, and anybody else who happens to be in the way. In a letter he explains, *I am not insane. I'm simply very angry.*

I know how he feels. He wants it all back the way it was before everything broke in two. He wants a clean well-lighted place, an African-free Africa. He wants a world where there's Pat Boone but no Little Richard. Where there's an Elvis but not the real one.

But there's also no memory of a four-year-old daughter standing in the doorway waiting for him to come home. There is no woman who tells him after twenty years that she will stand in this fire no matter what goes up in flames.

Heat comes out of the shit, Arnie Mindell says to me at a workshop one day; how can you hope to cook without heat? Life itself is the *prima materia*. Whatever's there the alchemist cooks, be it pleasant or awful.

Tree and leaf to mulch and peat, mulch and peat to soil and coal, coal to shining diamond. We're pure carbon at last.[4]

Today, however, I do not want this burning. I want to be Wally, not that trickster Eddie Haskell. I want to sing "Memories Are Made Of This" just the way Elvis' mother likes.

I do not want these words, this wife, this body or this life. I do not want what the gods bring.

※

If a solution remains undisturbed as it is cooled, I read, it may pass the point at which it would normally crystallize. If, however, a tiny seed is added to the substance, a sudden chain reaction occurs.

When combustion is complete, chemistry teaches, there is no ash.

※

After a while Gladys didn't even want Elvis to sing. She didn't like the way those girls screamed and shook when he stood there with his old guitar and started to shimmer like a wave of heat. She feared for the boy, but more deeply it was the boy himself she feared. She knew he'd moved beyond her. For two and a half minutes he'd found the solution to the body.

Elvis heads us off at the pass. With a quick twist he cuts open everything that moves.

※

I dreamed last week that my wife held a match to my hair and watched the gold of that sky turn red and blue with flames. As the roof went up in smoke I heard beautiful lines float down through the air—snatches of Sappho and Catallus, of Dante and Baudelaire. I heard Jimmie Rogers and Johnny Cash, Waylon Jennings and Jimmie Dale Gilmore. I saw my own tiny arms flailing inside a sterile hospital room, my hands as empty as an old bottle of bourbon. I saw all the space that surrounded my little astronaut body.

※

Walking among the Fires

As a teenager, my father tells me, he would come home from work and hear the sound of his mother's saxophone through the apartment window. It was the Depression. My grandfather, a classically trained pianist, was working the linotype machines or wasn't working at all so my grandmother had to fuck with the grocer every week just to put food on the table. Sometimes she would grow tired of the way her body felt and she would take the sax out of its case as if it were a knife. She would slice open the walls around her, try to break the mirror of her life into a million pieces.

I sometimes imagine how it must have sounded, something so beautiful flying through the air before turning again to ash.

Even now, so many years later, I can almost hear her cry, as though I too had been born inside that sound, as though it took on human form in me, passing like light through a darkened room. That sound would kneel at her feet like Gabriel. It was the beat of a wing approaching from another world.

Have you heard the news?

I like to imagine my grandfather in his final years reading about obscure alchemists from dusty books in the Chicago Public Library. Boehme and Paracelsus, Pico della Mirandola and Ficino, who wrote: *Whoever discovers his own genius through the means we have stated will thus find his own natural work, and at the same time he will find his own star and daimon.*[5]

Reading, he says to me, is a curious act of reflection. The mirror of the mind intensifies the light until it sets the very leaves you read on fire.

Christ, he says to me, is an incubator. He's the charnel ground: both womb and tomb, two doors to the same house. He's the question and retort. Then he'd explain about that closed vessel used by alchemists for sublimation and distillation, which uses heat to purify, vaporizing alcohol from water and then cooling it through condensation.

Poetry, Gwendolyn Brooks called it: a thing distilled.

I think often these days about my Scandinavian grandfather, who traveled about Nebraska in the 1920's giving concerts, played jazz in Chicago, read seven languages but never had the money to leave the country, working all day in the dust and oil of the printing press only to go home to read Sophocles, sitting with a glass of gin and his pack of Lucky Strikes.

Like my grandmother, he was raised as a Seventh Day Adventist. Like her, he died of emphysema.

The stuff my grandparents distilled in the 1920's was essentially the same that traders sold to the Indians shortly before my great grandparents arrived in the Midwest—what came to be called *firewater*. Obtained by a simple and inexpensive process of fermenting the sugars and starches in grain, it produces a colorless, volatile, and very flammable liquid, C_2H_5OH.

The word *alcohol* comes to us from the Arabic by way of the alchemists. *Whiskey* is from the Irish *usquebaugh*, from the Gaelic *uisce beathadh*, meaning *"water of life."*

It's a beautiful thing, both burning and subtle. *A good familiar creature,* as Iago would say, *if it be well used.*

According to the old alchemists, it takes the presence of Hermes to make the alchemical process cook. Both angel and trickster, he's famous for playing both sides of the law. He's guardian of the crossroads, guide to the underworld, and inventor of poetry's tools—the lyre and the alphabet. He's Memory's opposite, Jane Hirshfield reminds us. Her power "is primarily in service of conservation and continuance. The power of Hermes is that of change."[6]

He's how we cross over. Language heated into metaphor becomes crystal, a tool for cutting doors between worlds.[7] It's a diamond blade, Will's subtle knife.

The poem, I'm thinking, is a holy vessel; it's a rich and brutal retort. This furnace of language becomes healing waters: *Shantih, Shantih, Shantih.*

It's an old story. This burning building of a world is a door.

Walking among the Fires

6

Judy and I wake up on a Saturday morning, a week later in September, the sense of a weekend buried beneath the weight of everything that needs to be done. The house is unfinished, dust and dirt crammed with us into one room upstairs along with my books which are piled at the end of the bed around my dresser.

We look at each other and laugh. We're black fire on white fire. Like Hansel and Gretel, everyday inside this witch's oven we burn a little brighter. Just by standing in it we grow clearer, a little more brilliant around the edges.

I like to imagine them years later: Hansel might try to forget it all down at the tavern but at night Gretel takes those memories and distills them into songs, a few simple notes. *I went down to the crossroads*, begins one. They're a blade in her hands; every night she returns home ecstatic and bloodied.

She takes her rage and swallows it down. She watches it all cook inside the sweet retort of her body.

Schweigen, she sings, *wie Gold gekocht, in / verkohlten / Handen.*
Silence, cooked like gold, in / charred / hands.[8]

Every day she walks away from her home and threads her way up the pass. For three hours she sits in the gap in those mountains opening her body to the sun's stony blade. She drinks again at that witch's sweet and fiery tit, swallowing everything that thief taught her.

At 3:00 PM she goes home. She works in the garden, paints, writes long letters to her father and does the housework. By the time Hansel returns dinner is ready, the dishes washed, and a cold glass of sauvignon blanc—dry and chalky—is on the table.

She washes the evening dishes, looking out the small kitchen window to the woods beyond as her hands glide through the warm water. The body, she knows, is a dark forest. It's dense and beautiful with limbs and trunk, with swamps and pools and rivers of blood.

She kneels there at the delta, a seed of carbon, of light.

At night she dreams of a voice that breaks her insides like emergency glass. She's a match struck in a dark cave. She's the oil inside the bridesmaid's lamp. He's the very air that ignites her.

Rising the next morning she bathes as the organ at the church begins its closing hymn, the sound dissolving into the ringing of bells.

> What is this Light so fair, so tender
> Breaking upon our wond'ring eyes
> Never the Morning Star so radiant
> Followed his course o'er eastern skies

The stone of her body turns liquid. She is molten gold beneath him. She is the unsealed letter, an infinite and holy sonnet. She's the library of Alexandria burning.

My mother calls from Florida. The temperature of the Gulf is above 90° F, so warm it becomes impossible to tell where the body stops and all that water begins. My father swam this morning, then they watched Princess Diana's funeral. There's a cool breeze through the back bedroom window. Did I hear that 120 manatees had died along the coast? No one knows why. Maybe red tide, my mother says. Maybe, I'm thinking, terminal loneliness.

As I listen I sit at my grandfather's old desk in my daughter's room, the only space free for the computer with the house still under construction. The window is open. Lloyd pounds in long strips of cedar siding just a few feet away while Jay runs the saw in what's left of the yard. The dog lies at my feet, his right leg in a long green splint. Our car is no longer running.

It's easy for me to imagine where my mother is as she talks. The apartment is cooled by the Gulf in spite of the September heat. The sliding glass doors are open to the porch; pelicans catch the breeze between buildings and soar just feet outside their windows.

I know that place well, having visited the coast every winter since I was in high school. I know about the landing of de Soto a few miles to the north, and of Ponce de Leon. I know that as early as the sixteenth century the Franciscans had replaced the Spanish Jesuits, proselytizing and establishing trading posts among the Timucua people, who were placed in a kind of indentured servitude, controlled by the missions and paid little or nothing for their goods. I know that they were beaten and then killed off by various forms of burning: smallpox, yellow fever, typhus. Less than twenty years after the arrival of the Franciscans three quarters of the central and northern Florida natives had been wiped out by fevers.

I hang up the phone. My fingers run over the old maple of my grandfather's desk. Some of the handles to the drawers are missing, and the wood, while still beautiful, is badly scratched and stained.

I'm remembering how yesterday over a shared double tall mocha Judy explained to me how frightened she is to be leaving her old job, how uncertain she is of my support. She's thinking, she said, about how we separated when she started her first year of law school, and separated again the day after she took the Bar.

There is, I was thinking as she talked, something about the law that I must not like. I do not say this. I do not need to.

But for the first time, really, I understand something of how it must have felt watching her father die when she was five. It was like watching me leave over and over again.

What can I say? I taste a little of what burns in both of us far below the surface, what we've feared all along. A mighty river of fire.

Earth is a crucible, I'm thinking. Writing is a crucible. Marriage is a crucible.

There are great currents we move within, great possibilities. If gravity had its way, as one writer says, it "would soon run all the water into the lakes and seas, and then smooth them out like sheets of glass."[9] Heat on the other hand stirs things up. Rub any two people together and friction results. Molecules begin to vibrate, desperate to get away from each other. They need a little more space so they put in twin beds, then a room above the garage; they build a cabin by the lake.

None of it helps. Eventually with enough pressure the very forms change: molecules break apart, becoming something else entirely.

It's the 21st of September. I'm listening to Sequentia sing old Troubadour music, to Earl downstairs scraping away at nail holes, priming us for another paint job. Judy is at the office. My folks are in their apartment, the blinds pulled against the intense sunlight that floods in from the windows that cover the entire outside walls of the condominium.

On Tuesday when my father went in for a chest X-ray they found a dark spot on the lung. I talked to him last night, after a CAT scan was done, and he began telling me about Jerry Fallon, an old friend with whose son I played baseball as a kid. Jerry went in for an exam a month ago and was dead of lung cancer three weeks later.

I sit on the stairs, holding the phone and waiting.

My news, he said, is pretty good compared to that.

Well, I'm saying, you'd be hard put to make it worse.

They're calling it bronchiectisis; fluid collects in the lung and has to be expelled. It won't kill me, at least not for a while—and what the hell, I'm seventy-five.

So it's good news.

Yes. But you know, he adds, whenever something like this comes up it makes you think. But I always have a hard time praying for any specific result. Mostly I just hope for the strength to deal with whatever it is. Just to take it.

Yes, I say. Whatever the truth is.

We hang up and I sit there a moment, looking at the sunlight on the old fir floors, on the bare walls.

I remember a conversation with a friend who had recently witnessed the death of her mother. Amazingly, what she felt at the time was not simply grief but a kind of ecstasy. There was something there that was utterly simple, something we spend our lives seeking and avoiding. It was the truth. Reality had a hold of her.

I remember Romolus Linney's story, one I've often told on retreats, a story my father would like. It's about an apothecary who goes to Jesus seeking help for his dying father, to whom he has devoted his entire life. Jesus tells him to put his father in the oven, bake him for three hours, then take him out. He does this and then runs back to Jesus to describe what happened.

"I sat in front of that oven for three hours. It was awful. I heard cracking sounds. My father's bones, burning. Then, after three hours, I heard whistling. Then singing."

That old oven fires the father up.

"My father jumped off the baking sheet. He dressed himself up. I had to chase him all over town. He said the most horrible things. He got drunk with the blacksmith, insulted the mayor, and made indecent proposals to five women and a ten-year-old boy. It's impossible."

Jesus nodded. "I understand."

"Thank you Lord," said the Apothecary. "But what am I going to do now?"

"Your father will get sick again," said Jesus. "If doctors can't cure him forget your medicines, and mine, and let him go."

"Go?"

Jesus nodded.

"Can I do that?"

Jesus nodded.

"There's nothing wrong with that?"

"No," said Jesus. "You can get married and be a father yourself. There's nothing wrong with that, either."

"Really?" said the Apothecary, stunned. "Just—let—him—"

"Go," said Jesus, very quietly.[10]

I remember being thirteen, lying in front of the fire on a dark winter night, the big living room radio tuned to WSDM-FM as I read Robert W. Service. My folks are dressed up for a cocktail party. The smell of Chanel No. 5 hangs in the air; the dog lies beside me. I open up the old book of my grandmother's, passed on to me by my mother, and read the inscription: *To Gladys—May we always be as happy as we are tonight. Alvin. June 23, 1920.*

I turn another page and begin to read.

> There are strange things done in the midnight sun
> By the men who moil for gold;
> The arctic trails have their secret tales
> That would make your blood run cold;
> The Northern Lights have seen queer sights,
> But the queerest they ever did see
> Was that night on the marge of Lake Lebarge
> I cremated Sam McGee.

Rapture of the Deep

I remember the heat of that fire on my face as I lay on my stomach and read those words. I remember too the sweetness of heat as we drove south to Florida year after year in the 1950's, leaving behind the snows of Chicago, rolling down Highway 41 to Nashville in a single day. We were retracing history, following the river back to where the world began. Memphis and Muscle Shoals, Sun Records, that Studio on Union Street that Elvis walked into one day and came back out a god, a beautiful burning lamb.

Have you heard the news? There's good rockin' tonight.

I'm three-years-old as we pass by that building for the first time; Elvis is 21. He may have been somewhere near by, having coffee with a girl after ripping it up in the studio. My head is resting in my father's lap as he drives, my legs draped across my mother who sits with the map and a thermos of Maxwell House. My brother sleeps stretched across the back. There is no interstate, no Holiday Inn, no MacDonald's.

My mother turns the radio dial and picks up a snatch of Chuck Berry.

Long distance information
Give me Memphis Tennessee
Help me find the party
That's trying to get in touch with me

She turns to static and scattered signals all across the dial: Hank Williams and Ernest Tubb, Eddy Arnold and Roy Acuff. Sinatra. Sister Rosetta Tharpe and B.B. King. The Louvin Brothers on WMPS. The air itself changes as we travel from state to state, as we roll on down through Kentucky and Tennessee, finally smelling the orange groves and the salt of the sea. The sun burning. The cold waves burying us.

I cannot part from Love, Sequentia sings, for *Love has taken hold of me . . . by means of the one look which consumes my heart, sent by the one who inflames me.*

Well since my baby left me
I've found a new place to dwell
I'm down at the end of Lonely Street
at Heartbreak Hotel

Love, the beautiful young Elvis sings, is an invisible sun, an eternal combustion engine. It's a great burning ball of fire, a billion year old chemical reaction. A quick flick of the hips.
Just this.

Princess Diana's funeral attracted—by some estimates—something like three million people to London, making it the largest such event in history.

Here in Seattle the memorial service at the Episcopal cathedral brought out close to three thousand. Days later, flowers overflowed the entryway, and a table was still set up with a beautiful photo surrounded by burning candles and offerings. Saint Diana.

I didn't go. Instead I walked up the hill to Woodland Park and listened to Rosanne Cash sing about rising from the ashes, about the flame in our souls never burning out. "I'll send the angels to watch over you tonight," she sang.

> And you send them right back to me
> A lonely road is a bodyguard
> If we really want it to be
> There's fascination behind every window
> But I know you really care for me
> And soon we'll be sleeping in Paris
> And we can set those angels free

7

As *The Subtle Knife* ends, angels—*bene elim* they call themselves—come for Will, ready to take him to Lord Asriel, Lyra's father. They have followed the shaman, Will's father, to find the boy, and now that shaman has done his work and died. *There is a war coming, boy,* his father has said to him. *Something like it happened before, and this time the right side must win. We've had nothing but lies and propaganda and cruelty and deceit for all the thousands of years of human history. It's time we started again, but properly this time. . . .*

We finish the book at home, a month out of the mountains, at the solstice.

Rapture of the Deep

That night I dream that I'm sitting in a swing high up in the narrow branches of a Douglas Fir. Four ravens are slowly unraveling the ropes that hold the swing in place, tugging patiently at the threads with their beaks as I watch. I get out. Judy gets out. We get out together.

Lloyd pounds on the wall outside. Now The Tallis Scholars sing Josquin, the women's voices soaring like fish, rising through rivers of air.

> Kyrie eleison
> Christe eleison
> Kyrie eleison

I'm forty-four-years-old, a teacher, a father, and sometimes a spiritual director, which only means that others come to me because I don't seem to have all the answers. They come to me like a gap in the wall, a narrow pass through the mountains. They come, as my daughter said about hiking, because they want to see what's on the other side of things.

They don't know that all through the night these fires go on burning. I'm like one of those old Standard Oil refineries my mother's father worked at in Hammond Indiana, the flames eternally lighting up the night. I'm like Elvis, shaking like a leaf on a tree.

I sit here thinking about my father's parents, both dead years ago from voluntary inhalation of smoke. Great musicians both, trying to survive tough times. I think about my mother's parents, so fiercely German, burning with unspoken rage somewhere beneath the frozen ground. I think of my own mother and father, of my wife and thirteen year old child. I multiply the little I know by the number of human beings on the planet until it becomes a mighty fire of pain blowing the planet clean.

As a boy I spent long winter nights brooding in my room, reading and writing, listening for some sound from another world. Waiting for something down there to hatch.

I was Lazarus, hoping and fearing that the moment to rise would pass.

But I myself was the door. It cannot pass without me. It will, like love, wait for me forever.

The music ends. Heat comes on in the house; I can hear it whistling through the vents in the wall. Soon I must get up to run the dog. Soon

Walking among the Fires

I leave to pick up Katie at school; a few hours later and Judy comes home. Dinner and another evening putting fresh paint on new walls.

I put away Josquin in favor of the beautiful Ruth Brown, fondly remembering those old red and black Atlantic 45s of my adolescence, now gathering dust in the basement. Petroleum refined into black plastic discs. Music like walking a high mountain ridge. Like driving forever on a full tank of gas.

> Somebody touched me in the dark last night
> somebody moved me with all his might
> thrilled my soul when he held me tight
> ooh, ooh, ooh, in the dark last night

Rapture of the Deep

NOTES

1 *The Subtle Knife* (New York: Knopf, 1997). All subsequent quotations are from this edition.

2 The Dante translations (from *Purgatorio* 27 and 30) are by Allen Mandelbaum (New York: Bantam, 1982).

3 *Freude, shoner, Gotterfunken* . . . from the Ode to Joy, Beethoven's adaptation from Schiller in the final movement of his Ninth Symphony.

> Joy, o wondrous spark divine,
> Daughter of Elysium,
> Drunk with fire now we enter
> Heavenly one, your holy shrine.
> Your magic powers join again
> What fashion strictly did divide;
> Brotherhood unites all men
> Where your gentle wing's spread wide.
> [Translation: Clive Williams]

4 Arnie Mindell: see his *Sitting in the Fire* (Portland, Oregon: Lao Tse Press, 1995).

5 Ficino is quoted in Thomas Moore, *The Planets Within: The Astrological Psychology of Marsilio Ficino* (1982; rpt. Hudson, New York: The Lindisfarne Press, 1990) p. 55.

6 Jane Hirshfield, *Nine Gates: Entering the Mind of Poetry* (New York: HarperCollins, 1997), p. 186.

7 Compare Thomas Moore, *The Planets Within* p. 153; see also Hirshfield, *Nine Gates* 167: "It's as if such poets are holding a knife by the blade while they write."

8 Paul Celan, "Chymish," translated, "Alchemical," in *The Poems of Paul Celan*, translated by Michael Hamburger (New York: Persea Books, 1995), p 183.

9 If gravity had its way . . . Anne Botsford Comstock, *Handbook of Nature Study* (1911; rpt. New York: Cornell University Press, 1967), p. 792.

10 Romulus Linney, *Jesus Tales* (San Francisco: North Point Press, 1987), pp. 69–70.

Interlude

Shadows on the Land

> *The woods were already filled with shadows one June evening, just before eight O' clock, though a bright sunset still glimmered faintly among the trunks of the trees. A little girl was driving home her cow, a plodding, dilatory provoking creature in her behavior, but a valued companion for all that. They were going away from the western light, and striking deep into the dark woods, but their feet were familiar with the path, and it was no matter whether their eyes could see it or not . . .*
> —Sarah Orne Jewett,
> "The White Heron"

It's a simple story. Sylvia, nine years old, experiences a subtle sexual awakening in her attraction for a strange young man; as Jewett puts it, "the woman's heart, asleep in the child, was vaguely thrilled by a dream of love." But when the young man, an ornithologist, asks her to show him the nest of the beautiful heron, she turns shy as a bird herself. She has seen it, yes, but will say nothing to the stranger. Instead, in the predawn darkness she seeks for its nest alone, climbing the great pine tree, "the last of its generation," and rises above the shadows in order to get a bird's eye view. In doing so, in risking herself to share the bird's own perspective, she achieves an initiation into new knowledge—but not through the young man, through the heron. For her patience, her diligence, and her good heart, the reward is this vision of the nest "while the dawn grew bright in the east."

She has penetrated to the source; "she knows his secret now. "But will she tell the young man, who wishes to shoot the bird to add it to his collection? What will she do with her hard-won knowledge? To whom does she owe allegiance?

The woods are filled with shadows. It's an old story, older by far than those dark tales of Hawthorne, old even by Dante's time. Shadows lurk in this world; darkness always approaches.

Shadows on the Land

And yet this story, which begins so conspicuously with shadows, immediately sets out to re-educate us. Whatever might be foreboding in that opening clause is quickly eliminated: these shadows are *familiar*, as safe as that old cow. Sylvia is at home in these woods, as her name would suggest (from the Latin *silva*, woods, as in Dante's *selva oscura*). She walks through this valley of shadows and is not afraid.

Curiously, the significant (as in symbolic) shadow of the story belongs not to the literal level—the woods—but to the figurative shadow the young man casts. He, ironically, is the one "foreshadowed" here—a literary term so familiar to us that we miss its literal thrust, its shadowyness. And this, in a sense, is Jewett's point: the literal shadows of the trees are not the shadows we need to worry about. Instead, it turns out, the enemy is us.

In a further irony, the shadow this young ornithologist throws is what we have for so long seen as our primary source of light: the human ability to analyze, dissect, and understand. This is why our young man has come into the woods: he shoots birds in order to study, to list and define. He comes to bring his own kind of light.

How did such a reversal come to be? If we begin with the dictionary definition of "shadow," we may approach an answer: my old American Heritage begins by calling the shadow "an area that is not, or is only partially irradiated or illuminated because of the interception of radiation by an opaque object between the area and the source of radiation." This scientific definition—given pride of first place in the dictionary—brings a certain clarity; and yet such heavily Latinate language actually seems to *obscure* my sense of the word. As with our young Audubon-like ornithographer, the very act of illuminating this shadow by defining it comes close to destroying it—or *de-storying* it.

Such information is certainly useful; I've consulted the dictionary (not to mention the Audubon books) with great pleasure. And yet I come back wanting a little more *shadow*, more depth. All of that direct analytical light seems to flatten things down to a single dimension. Not surprisingly, of course; after all, we know that shadows give us a sense of perspective. *Chiaroscuro: clarus /obscuros*. It's the very obscurity of the shadow that gives light its depth and meaning—and vice versa. It's the yin / yang of the Taoists, out of which life in all of its roundness is made.

Rapture of the Deep

Light alone reveals stunningly, but in the very act of revealing it can also distort, erasing the depths of those dark shadows. Light de-stories: it eliminates the *poetry* of things. Which is why, perhaps, Paul Celan writes

> Speak—
> But keep yes and no unsplit.
> And give your say this meaning:
> give it the shade.

He speaks truly who speaks the shade, Celan writes. A survivor of Hitler's concentration camps—another attempt to eliminate shadows—Celan speaks as one who knows that to "speak the shade" also means to summon ghosts, to call up the unseen and unspoken, which may finally turn out to be the physical world itself.

Banish the shadow, we might say with Falstaff, and you banish all the world. Banish Fat Jack, Prince Hal's large shadow, and you banish weight, body, and earth. You banish the mess that life often is. You banish humor. And you wind up with that first, denotative definition of shadow, a definition that is itself shadowless. You find a forest without mystery, which is no forest at all.

They are rich in resonance, these shadows, rich in all they conjure. Shadows enchant, haunt, frighten and entice. They lurk and linger within us; they call our names out of the dark places in our souls. Their very presence in a story, as in life, brings mystery and depth. In doing so the shadows in our lives both follow *and* lead us, depending on whether we're heading into the light or—like John Donne on Good Friday—riding westward, with the rising Sun at our backs. But even as we turn away the very presence of our shadow before us may become a guide: the shadow itself will lead us home, if we let it. What else—in Tolkien's *Lord of the Rings*—but this hard truth is the lesson of the long journey of the faithful Sam and Frodo? Gollum, much hated, feared and pitied, is always present, *swiftly but warily creeping on behind, a slinking shadow among the stones.* Our eternal follower and guide, he's that darkness, that *earth*, we cannot shake, and cannot do without.

Chapter Four

Death Enters the Wilderness Singing

For we are the stars. For we wing.
For we sing with our light.
For we are birds made of fire.
For we spread our wings over the sky.
Our light is a voice.
We cut a road for the soul
for its journey through death.

An Eskimo story explains the origin of light as follows: 'in the eternal darkness, the crow, unable to find any food, longed for light, and the earth was illumined.' If there is a real desire, if the thing desired is really light, the desire for light produces it.

—Simone Weil[1]

1

Darkness gathers around. Out in the meadow in the middle of the night, wind blowing, the silhouettes of mountains on three sides of me, the stars blazing above: Cassiopeia, the Dipper. My daughter Katie and her cousin Rebecca are in the tent back among the trees. Judy is in the other tent, reading by flashlight.

We have been in the mountains four days now.

I lie on the grass, beside the lupine and paintbrush, the daisies and monkshood, and I place my hands upon my heart and breathe. I lie like the dead, my arms the wings of a butterfly, golden as a monarch. Then in the middle of my chest a stone rolls away. I do not know how else to explain this. The space has no boundaries. It opens like a door, a vault, a cave.

The earth is cold beneath me. My jacket grows damp. *The system is failing*, I hear from deep within; *this system is breaking down*. I do not know if it means my body or capitalism or the earth itself. I do not even know if there is any difference. I wonder what could possibly follow and I have no answer. But I know it's true. The system is breaking down.

I sit up, cross my legs, and briefly open my eyes. I find myself in the bottom of a dark bowl. I breathe quietly and look around at the immense sky. It could be the womb of the earth. I could be sitting here waiting to be born.

I describe this moment here as if it can be isolated, giving it some of the clarity of a snapshot. But I know that it was informed by what occurred earlier that afternoon as we climbed from Macalester Lake up to the Pass, when Katie was suddenly seized with sharp pains in her abdomen. I remember the look in her eyes, the tears which were not from pain but fear, which was only slightly relieved when her mother or I would assure her that certainly it was from the lunch and the tightness of the waist strap, it will pass, and then it didn't as we continued slowly up the trail and she had to stop again and again and I'm standing there on a very dusty trail ten miles in any direction from anything even remotely medical—or even human for that matter—and I'm thinking and I can tell as I look at Judy that she's thinking *appendicitis.*

And I'm remembering that Rebecca's father—my brother—had appendicitis just a few years ago that went undiagnosed and came close to killing him, and I'm calculating from my own appendectomy fourteen years ago just how long we can wait before taking some kind of action, and I'm trying to imagine just what that action might be. Assuming the worst I figure that I could make the ten miles or so down the mountain without a pack in a few hours and from there find someone who could radio for a helicopter that could fly in and land in the meadow easily enough and pick up Katie (and Judy? And Rebecca?) and carry her to a hospital in order to perform the appendectomy.

Except, of course, that we're in a National Wilderness Area, where, by law, no helicopters—no motors at all—are allowed.

In theory I've believed that wilderness areas (already something of an oxymoron) should be left, as much as possible, without human interference. I've also believed that the hard and fast rules around this idea miss the fact that humans are as much a part of the natural order as any other creature, and inevitably move about in "wilderness" areas just as wolves and bears do. Sometimes they make trails. They erect temporary structures.

And so it's not so simple.

What is simple is the realization that when you walk far enough outside your house you put yourself at risk. And that, in part, is the point.

At a loss for answers I told Katie I would walk up the trail to see how far we were from the pass, and if I reached it I'd come back for her pack. At that point I left the others and headed up the switchbacks alone, watching my feet move through the dust, my walking stick—christened "Will" by Katie the day before—thumping along with each step. I prayed, almost mechanically, until I suddenly found I'd reached the end of the switchbacks and could see the meadow ahead that signaled Macalester Pass. And at that point I stopped, as something altogether unfamiliar occurred to me: I thought of offering myself as an exchange, my life for my daughter's.

I stood there, my pack off, looking around the familiar landscape, under the heat of the midday August sun. One of my favorite places in the world, it was the first place Judy and I had taken Katie when we began these trips years ago. It was here I had heard wolves early one morning, and here, or just above it, where we'd awoken to snow one August morning. It was a place I loved, and yet for those few seconds I knew with utter clarity that I was ready to make that deal. I was ready to let it all go.

I went back to the others, slung on Katie's pack and together we hiked slowly up to the pass and on to Hidden Meadows, which we reached late in the afternoon. There we set up the tent and stove, found a tree to hang the food, and then finally relaxed, taking our camping towels and books out into the meadow. I watched my fourteen year old daughter read and dip her feet into the brook, the symptoms disappearing as the day passed into evening, amazed at how quickly we managed to reenter our normal life, and amazed—for a brief, naïve moment—that anyone should ever quarrel, given how fragile our hold on life is.

I sat in the sun reading William Stafford's *Allegiances,* a book which took me back to my final year in college, when I wasn't much older than Kate. I remember sitting in the classroom at Beloit as I watched David Stocking read the title poem, listening as I glanced out the open window and caught a little of the October breeze, the late Wisconsin light filtering through.

Rapture of the Deep

It is time for all the heroes to go home
if they have any, time for all of us common ones
to locate ourselves by the real things
we live by.

Far to the north, or indeed in any direction,
strange mountains and creatures have always lurked—
elves, goblins, trolls, and spiders:—we
encounter them in dread and wonder,

But once we have tasted far streams, touched the gold,
found some limit beyond the waterfall,
a season changes, and we come back, changed
but safe, quiet, grateful.

Suppose an insane wind holds all the hills
while strange beliefs whine at the traveler's ears,
we ordinary beings can cling to the earth and love
where we are, sturdy for common things.[2]

We come back I read again a quarter of a century later, sitting up there at 6,500 feet; *We come back, changed / but safe*. It's a poem about journeying—literally or figuratively—into places of wonder, but more deeply still it's about returning. Rather than focusing on the hero's journey, Stafford frames his poem with that word *common*, a word I had always misunderstood because I misunderstood all that common really holds. Too easily I moved to *cheap, average, of mediocre or inferior quality*, and missed the underlying truth of the word: *Belonging equally to two or more; joint; pertaining to the community as a whole*. I missed as well the underlying roots, which stretch all the way down through the Latin *communis* (leading not only to common but to *commune, communicate*) and the Old English *gemaene* (common, public, as in mean, demean) to the Indo European **mei*, which meant *to change, move, with derivatives referring to the exchange of goods and services within a society*.

This is what it means *to hold in common*. The word migrates from the underlying idea of motion, the process which produces change, and which leads to exchange and thence to related terms: the Latin *mutare*, for example, as in mutate, molt, commute, transmute; and *mutuus,* "done in exchange," as well as the Old English *gemad,* as in mad, insane—surely, as Stafford acknowledges, one of the risks of the journey. This all goes along with the Old English and Norse prefix *mis,* from the underlying Germanic root **missa-,* "in a changed manner," abnormally, wrongly, as in mistake.

It is the risk of wandering, and of wilderness: missing the way, making the mistake, driven mad by some insane wind. But this is exactly what leads to *transmute* and *mutate.* This is what happens when you travel with Hermes—known to the Romans as Mercury, from whom we get our word *commerce.* He's also our guide to the underworld, the one who leads us, through dread and wonder, back into community.

It is impossible, I'm suddenly realizing, to separate these "strange mountains" from "all of us common ones," just as it's wrong not to realize that those wandering heroes that Stafford writes of are *us.* Every exchange demands a journey, a tiny going forth. And this, the journey and the exchange—of goods, of ideas, of love—is precisely what keeps the common (and The Commons) alive.

Take Pentecost as an example. Tongues of flame, transformed speech: a hundred languages suddenly understood as something beneath each language is at last—or once again— held in common. Pentecost *creates* this community: it's the birth of the church precisely because it unites in the Spirit all that has been driven apart. All those infected by this insane wind realize that what they know together transcends class and race and gender: everything is born from this spirit of unending exchange, which is another name for love.

There is no other way to do it. Not, at least, on this planet.

2

A month after returning from the mountains with my family I find myself once again under the stars late at night, this time on a weeklong meditation retreat. Trying to sleep by burrowing deep in my bag, by 6:00 A.M. the gulls are in motion, heading west over the empty fields, in flight and rising against the blue sky.

I lie like a mummy. I breathe slowly, easily.

By Tuesday morning the meditation has become very simple. Just breath, concentration lightly on the heart center, some space that's there and not there.

We live, I'm thinking, in an ocean of air. I breathe in the body of this world atom by atom. I feel her sing beneath my feet. I feel her rising beneath me, her dawn and noon and night. Her quickness. The fluid of her form.

With every breath I climb the river of her.

It's hunger that sends us out into this wilderness on retreat, as it is hunger that we try to solve by figuring out ways to turn stones into bread—meaning that we seek ways to end this spiritual longing through means we can control: technology, ownership, material goods. This is the god that commerce too often serves. But this hunger will not be done away with so easily. It is our curse and it is our gift.

It shouldn't be surprising that so many creation stories have to do with food: Raven for example in some Northwest Indian tales creates the world out of his own hunger, and Hermes within a day of his birth is stealing the cattle of Apollo. And then there's the apple.

As Hermes says to his mother,

> I'm ready to do whatever I must so that you and I will never go hungry. . . . Why should we be the only gods who never eat the fruits of sacrifice and prayer? Better always to live in the company of the deathless ones—rich, glamorous, enjoying heaps of grain—than forever to sit by ourselves in a gloomy cave.[3]

"To eat meat," as Lewis Hyde summarizes, "is to be confined to the mortal realm." This is what occurs to Raven—and to Adam and Eve. Death is the result of eating. Eating is a mark of our mortality. Every moment of hunger is a faint reminder of our fall.

I know this from my own hunger. She is ancient and child-like and utterly demanding. I have known for years that she will devour me unless I learn to climb so deeply inside her that there is nothing at all of me left.

Only the holder the flag fits into, as Rumi says, and wind. No flag.

Truly I have been married to her. She has been my creature and I have been hers. She has taught me that beneath the literal death that comes of not eating is a deeper death that comes of eating mindlessly. And she taught me that beneath that fear of hunger lies real life, a place of authenticity and truth, of beauty and grace and forgiveness. She showed me that inside my hunger lie mountains and seas and a sky so huge it swallows even hunger itself.

She is beautiful, my hunger, as beautiful as the wind. What she builds has been hollowed out at the core. A flute, a saxophone, an empty honey jar. A home.

3

In the final meditation of the retreat Jerry, the Center's director, lies down in the center of the circle and says: meditate my death. Meditate my corpse.

We sit in the circle around his form, close our eyes, and breathe in his end. We come to the point. We imagine him gone, *sunyata*, a big zero.

Where, I wonder, does it go? That last breath and the person—*something*—gone. That finality of stone.

Earth, Water, Fire, Air. This beautiful July day, the sky blue and deep like an open door.

We meditate Jerry's death, which is simply to meditate his absence, and to meditate our own. But what in the face of this eternal presence is *absence*? The body itself becomes a koan. *It will be nailed up* it says *but don't think you can't walk through.*

We meditate in silence, the front door open, a cool breeze blowing in off the water. We enter the cave of the body and go down. We seek Eurydice. We follow Hermes. A stairway winds down through the pharynx, the trachea, the lungs and diaphragm, the heart space in the center. Time flies and the meditation deepens. We climb down inside this beautiful body, we breathe its rhythms flung from far inside its lyric space. It's a little room in Jerusalem. We're held in common inside its beautiful emptiness. It sings us. The wind whispers *holy, holy, holy.*

4

While it may seem odd, there is a reason that the psychologist Carl Jung and others have associated Jesus with the Trickster, and have seen in the trickster tales the origins of sacrifice. In the story of Hermes stealing Apollo's cattle, for example, Hermes chooses not to eat the cattle but instead to "offer it up" as *sema*, as sign. His act is mirrored in the cross, only this time it is the Trickster himself who is raised up, and whose own body becomes, eucharistically, a sacrifice "for the whole world." This doesn't mean that through some vague "belief" in Jesus we are mysteriously saved from our sins. It means that Jesus as sign gives us a chance to see the underlying truth of the universe. Here's reality: not simply in turning food into ourselves but in turning ourselves into food. *Take eat, this is my body.*

As Jung summarizes, our deepest self "demands sacrifice by sacrificing itself to us."[4]

Jesus' work begins, the gospels tell us, as he is called by the Spirit into the wilderness, where, in a sense, he comes to know himself as a kind of crossroads. Here he is open to the elements. His experience is the opposite of those who go into the wilderness in order to conquer it. What he conquers is himself, and he does it by dying *to* himself. He walks off the map, both literally and figuratively. In doing so he comes back to himself, knowing himself as "Son."

He knows himself as that place of exchange.

His restraint in the desert recalls Hermes' restraint around the meat: it is the restraint of the ego to some greater force than its own immediate well-being and safety. While on one level it is the resistance of appetite, it is not in the end a rejection of appetite: it is instead a profound recognition of its meaning, which is located in a far deeper wilderness than we normally perceive. Appetite, desire—all that goes by the name of *Eros*—will carry us right to the source of that hunger if we listen to it deeply enough. That listening is the meaning of wilderness.

This is not some willful asceticism; it is not eating and yet remaining alive and open to the reality of hunger. We know in this place our own radical vulnerability and poverty; we know, most deeply, the reality of death. We deny nothing of this mystery. And in our openness in this wilderness we suddenly discover our freedom: we're as large as this space around us: this sea, this desert, these mountains. Our desire is our road, our way and our truth.

If Jesus "knows the father" directly, he does so because in the wilderness he has gone directly to the source of hunger and now knows himself as one with it. He *is* that desert. Knowing himself as unbounded space, he will not be satisfied with substitutes.

The mistake the church often makes is to assume that Jesus saves (himself and others) by repressing this desire, and thus by denying the wild. But Jesus does not stay away from life, as his association with prostitutes and drinkers (and tax collectors—the kin of Hermes!) would suggest; he is himself the very essence of that energy out of which all things are formed.

The answer, then, is not simply to eliminate the hunger by no longer eating (in other words, literally killing ourselves by denial). As we know, not eating can be as much an addiction as overeating. Instead the answer is to let the hunger become a road. It leads us through our drives into the wilderness, where we find we are one with the source of those drives.

What Jesus does in his actions is to show us another relationship with that force, a way of letting *it* use *us* instead of the other way around. The paradox is that as long as we attempt to manipulate and control that energy we inevitably remain its prisoner: that force will take the form of sin, and its drive will drive us crazy. Only when we surrender ourselves to the true underlying force will we discover ourselves free within it, because we are no longer fighting with our own essential nature, which arises *from* that force.

It is who we are.

From this perspective a fair definition of hell might be: anything to which we cling.

Jesus in this sense solves the mystery of hunger.

This solution is what the gospels are about. It's not surprising, then, to see how often Jesus' own story involves food. He walks out of the desert to turn water into wine for a wedding feast. This miracle at Cana is simply the first of many signs of who this God really is: He is himself the feast. He is that wine. Love lives to be eaten, to be taken in, to be tricked and broken and pounded down only to rise again. The feeding of the five thousand and the Last Supper (not to mention the cross and resurrection) merely confirm what has already been revealed. Rooted in the Jewish Passover ceremony and thus in the wilderness journey of the Exodus, this final feast sums up what life has meant all along.

In Rilke's words, "Move through transformation:"

If drinking is bitter, change yourself to wine.[5]

5

The meditation finally ends—I'm the timekeeper—and Jerry slowly sits up. We all joke but underneath we each know something about that cave that had a rock rolled up before its door. Already it's empty. It will always be empty.

Jerry goes home at the end of the week to discover that within his immediate circle of friends and parishioners there have been a dozen deaths. At summer camp a pal of Anne's—my friend Laurie's daughter—was hit by a falling tree and died. The father of a woman about to be married died. Another friend committed suicide.

In the Sudan the deaths come so fast no one can keep up. In Burundi and Rwanda. In the U.S.

Back east and down south all the air is sucked out by the heat. The flames devour us like the tongues of snakes, they feed on the air until there's nothing left to breathe. The nation's one huge fire sale. Everything goes up.

At a board meeting this morning four of us who had been on the retreat talk about our experiences, and our sense of what lies ahead. The U.S. manages to survive, but Diane reminds us that we're all tied into this single knot of fire. Eastern Europe, Asia and Russia, the Middle East. We're married to them all.

And so? Jerry asks. Do we take what little the corporation has and hide it under the mattress? Or do we simply do what we've been doing all along?

We climb deeper.

We stay in touch.

6

We live and die in community, I'm remembering, *sturdy for common things*. We are, whether we like it or not, roped together.

On how many nights have I stared out at the waves or mountains or up into the darkness of the sky and felt how true it is that we are made from and for this place. We evolve from it and with it, held in common with all of creation.

We are humus; we are stardust.

The Kingdom, it may turn out, is located down at the crossroads, that place of exchange where, Victor Turner reminds us, dwell those who "are neither here nor there; they are betwixt and between the positions assigned and arrayed by law, custom, convention, and ceremonial." This place "is frequently likened to death, to being in the womb, to invisibility, to darkness, to bisexuality, to the wilderness."[6]

As I watched my daughter soaking her feet in that mountain stream beneath the late afternoon sun, I remembered my own moment just a few hours before when, however briefly, I had made my own life into a crossroads. And as I looked around this mountain meadow, feeling—temporarily—so safe, I realized that here too is a crossroads, a place of unending exchange of light and water, seed and soil. But that crossroads is not so much a place as a *way*. Far streams and mountains, the city and its suburbs—it's all the same dance. None of us stays put. This place transforms, evolves, transmutes; it's a form of exchange, a kind of commerce. We carry each other around like credit cards; it's impossible to leave home without us. Impossible to leave at all.

We're mercury, quicksilver, flashes in the pan.

Let the wild rumpus start said the great god Hermes, and so it did, and it was good. It was history and so are we.

It's right that Hermes should be a wind god. He's another version of that Holy Spirit who moves through Pentecost: "the scribe of the gods and the divinity of wisdom, inventor of language, of words which bind and unbind." He "makes the souls to breathe."[7]

He's the wild thing who makes my heart sing. He makes everything. It's beneath his sign that I write.

Rapture of the Deep

NOTES

1 Epigraphs: *For we are the stars* is taken from a Passamauoddy poem, quoted in the liner notes to Jan Garbarek's recording *Rites*, ECM 1685/86. Simone Weil, *Waiting for God* (Harper Collins, 1951), p. 107.

2 Stafford, "Allegiances," in *Stories That Could Be True: New and Collected Poems* (Harper & Row, 1977) p. 193.

3 The stories about Hermes are drawn from Lewis Hyde, *Trickster Makes This World* (New York: North Point Press, 1998).

4 Jung, "Transformation Symbolism in the Mass," in *Collected Works* vol. 11, trans. R.F.C. Hull (Princeton: Princeton University Press, 1977), par. 400, p. 263, quoted in Robert Aziz, *C.G. Jung's Psychology of Religion and Synchronicity* (Albany: State University of New York Press, 1990), p 21.

5 Rilke, from *Sonnets to Orpheus*, translated by Stephen Mitchell (Simon & Schuster, 1985) p. 129.

6 Victor Turner, *The Ritual Process* (Aldine Publishing, 1969), p. 95, quoted in Marion Woodman, *The Pregnant Virgin* (Inner City Books, 1985), pp. 88–9.

7 Frances A. Yates, *Giordano Bruno and the Hermetic Tradition* (University of Chicago, 1964), pp. 2, 48.

Interlude

The Shadow, the Twins, and the Mall of America

Though I walk through The Mall of America
I Shall Fear No Evil
For with Time and Plastic in my Pocket
There's Nothing to FEAR Anyway.
—Sweatshirt for sale
at The Mall of America

What you fear will not go away: it will take you into yourself and bless you and keep you. That's the world, and we all live there.
—William Stafford

Constructed in America's northern heartland, just outside Minneapolis, on prairie land more recently covered by a stadium (before the Twins wimped out and moved indoors), the Mall is more than just another place to shop. 1,500 bus tours were booked in 1992, with 3,000 anticipated for 1994; 200,000 Japanese visitors are expected within a few years, and half a million Canadians. The Mall occupies over 4 million square feet of land, covering seventy-eight acres, most of which is filled with 350 retailers and, of course, the 13,000 free parking spaces.

Exchange is the blood of the place: *commerce,* after all, shares etymological roots with Mercury, the gods' tricky messenger, patron of merchants, travelers and thieves. And the association fits: everything's quicksilver here, all flash and motion, a whirl of ceaseless change. In this it mirrors America, producing a bountiful image of ourselves, which millions literally buy into. (My own university retirement fund owns a piece of this rock).

With its maze-like circularity, the design of the place gives the dizzying impression of an infinite sequence of stores, food, and games, all whirling about the hub of "Knott's Camp Snoopy," a massive seven-acre indoor amusement park. There are no straight lines, no clarity, no easy way from here to there. Instead, the entire point is distraction.

Even the escalators are designed not to provide quick access but instead to force the consumer to wander—passing, of course, as many shops as possible.

My wife and I have been reading Ursula Le Guin's *A Wizard of Earthsea* to our daughter during these Winter evenings, beginning and finishing around a holiday visit to family (and to the Mall) in Minnesota. We read of the Wizard Ged's apprenticeship, how through his adolescent pride and fear he brought forth out of the darkness a nameless shadow, his own dark twin. "All my acts have their echo in it," he tells a friend; "it is my creature."[1]

His painfully honest self-awareness comes to save him, and to distinguish him from others like him (Victor Frankenstein and Dr. Jekyll come to mind) who have also conjured up doubles, images of their own repressed desires. Like them, Ged has brought forth the one thing that he cannot control, since it embodies what he failed so miserably to face.

Like Victor Frankenstein, Ged's first impulse is to flee. It is only when he stops running that he sees that its strength lies precisely in his own fear of it. Even more, its creation presents him with the possibility of salvation, because for the first time he can see and own the fear and pride that had been there invisibly inside of him. Such is the power of metaphor: by embodying this shadow, he can turn and face it.

Victor Frankenstein never acknowledges his creature; instead he turns on it in rage, a failure which dooms him to a hopeless death in the frozen north. Ged too pursues his creature to earth's end, but learns instead that his fear can serve him, precisely because it is the thread that ties him to his shadowy twin. "At the sight of it," Le Guin writes, "fear had come into him again, the sinking dread that urged him to turn away, to run. . . . And he followed that fear as a hunter follows the signs, the broad, blunt clawed tracks of the bear, that may at any moment turn on him from the thickets."

It was odd indeed to recall Ged and Frankenstein under the bright artificial lights of America's largest Mall; as they wandered the dim seas and frigid poles I wandered in and out of clothing stores and fast food joints, all duplicating a dozenfold the same products. All seemed tame enough; and yet I kept thinking *there is a monster out there, and it has my face, my name.*

The Shadow, the Twins, and the Mall of America

And then it dawned on me: the monster is the Mall itself. Built with my money—all of our money—it rises around us as the great American projection, the rich consummation of all our mercurial dreams.

It is an odd and startling thought. Startling because on the surface of it the Mall seems anything but monstrous; indeed, we flock to its familiar stores by the millions just as we pour into Disney World and Hollywood, places famous for plastic-wrapping our fantasies. Here too there are no dark corners, except in carefully controlled rides in Camp Snoopy, where fears and shadows are manufactured and safe. The Minnesota cold is eliminated; the true mysteries of the night and stars do not enter.

It is as the sweatshirt jokes: *I will fear no evil.* The valley where the Twins once played under the open sky is now the massively enclosed mall where the twin—*myself*—is kept walled out. There is nothing to face—no shadows, no thickness, and no real depth. As in hell, all of the movement is mere facade: the place is endless static.

And yet I cannot shake the feeling as I wander the maze of corridors: *we have created a monster.* I can feel it everywhere I turn. No matter how many stores or movie screens distract us, no matter how much we spend: the bigger it is, the clearer the truth of our poverty grows. Our hunger grins back at us from the three-way mirrors that fill The Gap. These stores feed on us; they consume us by creating pale images of our profoundest needs: for love, security, and community; for nourishment and family; for soul.

We face this wall everywhere we turn. We long for life to be different, even as we fear the unknown that's inevitably lodged in that difference. We fear and long for change, and spend our days in a swirl (new clothes and cosmetics, new improved food and electronic gadgets) that mimics the genuine conversion we cannot bring ourselves to make. We prefer to stay in motion, afraid of being revealed. Moving targets are harder to hit.

Why can we not face our true longing? What is it that we dread? Call it an inner darkness, an unknown twin lost to us at birth. There is something down there that we both fear and desire; something hinted at in legends of dopplegangers and demons. So many stories whisper this truth to us—Tolkien's Gollum, the creature from the black lagoon. It's at home down there, it seems, a kind of host to a place we'd rather drain dry and pave over.

And still it calls to us in our dreams, taunts us and hunts us. It's both enemy and guide; we may hate it, but without it we are lost.

All of this is a way of naming what the Mall attempts to exclude, and what can never be excluded. In fact, what we have built here is a precise reflection of what we refuse to face.

The irony is great. In our attempts to wall out our longing we have done nothing but build a massive monument to it. But just as fear becomes a kind of light into Ged's deepest darkness, so too might this monster illuminate ours. If the Mall exists to house an endless series of images that pretend to satisfy our hunger, these same images—precisely because they are *reflections*—can lead us to their source deep within us. But to see this we must stand still and look. We must read these images backwards, as if they were all a familiar language written in a mirror.

This truth is underscored in James Hillman's comments about death and the underworld: "Rather than viewing the soul as expiating in a nightworld for our shady action in the dayworld," he writes, "we may imagine dayworld actions to be expiations for shadows we have not seen. As long as we act in the heroic mode, we are driven by guilt, always paying off. Our doings are more likely undoings, and our visible achievements are driven by an invisible image that either cannot rest (like Sisyphus ever on his hill) or cannot move (like Theseus stuck on his throne), because its desire can never be reached (like Tantalus' unslaked thirst)."[2]

What is it that moves us so? Sisyphus rolls his rock up the hill; Tantalus reaches to pluck the fruit from the ever-receding bough; and we—we shop till we drop. *Getting and spending,* the poet says, *we lay waste our powers.* We do not give ourselves away; we *spend* ourselves, forever missing the fruit—the *rest*—that seems to lie just ahead, with the next purchase. It is as Thich Nhat Hanh says: "Many people need a place to go before they realize that they do not have to go anywhere."[3]

Ged travels to the ends of the earth; the poet Kathleen Norris goes to—well, to Dakota. Same difference, one easily jokes. But it's true: both are places where one can be, as a monk there said, "alone with the Alone." Both are places where silence and solitude open up this hidden space inside us. And so both are places where this monstrous twin can be faced. "Ironically," Norris writes, "it is in choosing the stability of the monastery of the Plains, places where nothing ever happens . . . that we discover that we can change. In choosing a bare-bones existence, we are enriched, and can redefine success as an internal process rather than an outward display of wealth and power."[4]

This "outward display" is embodied in the Mall, which seems to rise up from the Midwestern plains as a sign of America's success. I fear, however, that it may be success only as Frankenstein's creation is: while he did indeed create it, he failed more deeply because he was never able to grasp its *meaning*. He never truly understood what drove him. He never stood still long enough to face what it could have told him about himself.

Perhaps for each of us there is a twin; like Oedipus, we may all be born with a truth we fear to face (our own death, if nothing else). And until that acceptance comes everything is darkened by it. Fear haunts our high-rise apartments, our elaborate alarms; it strides invisibly through the Mall, the uncrowned king of all it surveys.

It is this creature that forces itself upon Ged, and makes him determined at last to bring an end to his misery. "I am bound to the foul cruel thing," he knows, "and will be forever, unless I can learn the word that masters it: its name." He must discover what this shadow means to him—and, beyond him, to his world. This he does, as readers of *Earthsea* know. He stands before it at earth's end; "man and shadow met face to face."

> Aloud and clearly, breaking the old silence, Ged spoke the shadow's name and in the same moment the shadow spoke without lips or tongue, saying the same word: "Ged." And the two voices were one voice.
>
> Ged reached out his hands, dropping his staff, and took hold of his shadow, of the black self that reached out to him. Light and darkness met, and joined, and were one.

It should come as no surprise; it is always ourselves that we meet. Who else is it we fear in the face of the poor, the homeless? Who else should we see there but our Self? It is the Christ who says "I was hungry and you gave me food. I was a stranger and you welcomed me. . . . As you did it to the least of these my brethren, you did it to me."

Host and guest, we may recall, derive from the same etymological root. These two, the insider and outsider, are one.

"Ged had neither lost nor won," as the narrator reminds us; instead, "naming the shadow of his death with his own name, [he] had made himself whole."

"This thing of darkness I acknowledge mine," Prospero likewise says of Caliban at the end of *The Tempest,* and finds his freedom, his humanity, in the saying of it. There is nowhere else to go. The rest is pure mercy.

The Shadow, the Twins, and the Mall of America

NOTES

1 All quotations from *The Wizard of Earthsea* are from the Bantam (New York, 1975) edition.

2 James Hillman, *The Dream and the Underworld* (New York: Harper & Row, 1979) p. 57.

3 Thich Nhat Hanh, *For a Future To Be Possible* (Berkeley: Parallax Press, 1993) p.199.

4 Kathleen Norris, *Dakota: A Spiritual Geography* (New York: Ticknor & Fields, 1993) pp. 202–3.

Conclusion

Every time we sleep the contemplative awakens wearing robes of archetypal fire . . . every time the beautiful snags us and holds us momentarily in its embrace . . . in every instance where the presence of a loved one overflows the banks of the explainable . . . or our own solitude awakens in a desert where we stand naked alone in the divine presence. . . .
—James Finley, The Awakening Call

God's my life, stol 'n hence, and left me asleep! I have had a most rare vision. I have had a dream, past the wit of man to say what dream it was. Man is but an ass, if he go about t' expound this dream. . . . The eye of man hath not heard, the ear of man hath not seen, man's hand is not able to taste, his tongue to conceive, nor his heart to report, what my dream was. I will get Peter Quince to write a ballet of this dream. It shall be call'd "Bottom's Dream," because it hath no bottom
—Midsummer Night's Dream, IV. 1

1

The earth is the fruit of divine contemplation, a brooding over an abyss. Like Mary Magdalen, and like any true artist, God too watches over an empty tomb.

Contemplari, "to observe carefully," was originally a term of augury. *Templum,* from which the word contemplation stems, is the area in the sky (or on the ground) measured or cut out (Indo-European **tem*) by augurs for observation.[1]

It is likely that in its origins this word harkens back to a clearing away of the wild forests, which were thought to be profane because they obscured the sky, the source of divine signs. As Robert Harrison says: "Where divinity has been identified with the sky, or with the eternal geometry of the stars, or with cosmic infinity, or with 'heaven,' the forests become monstrous, for they hide the prospect of god."[2]

Conclusion

In this way the forest becomes the Other. It becomes, in Jung's sense, a kind of shadow: we project upon the darkening woods whatever darkness lies within us. And we then attempt to cure it by clear-cutting: in essence, by creating civilization, which is from this perspective nothing more than an attempt to see our way clear to the gods.

This is the genesis of both temple and city: open space bordered by a wilderness. A great cathedral (like a Greek temple) may be no more than the unconscious desire to replicate forest, with walls, flying buttresses, arches and stained glass windows recalling arching trees and filtered light. Which suggests, ironically, that it is when we are standing deeply within this forest that we feel most directly the presence of the divine. In the forest, as in the cathedral, we're reminded of our own smallness, our source in *humus*.[3]

Clear too much away and *humus* and holy vanish together: our own nature is gone, replaced by the dark blank of asphalt. We push back the borders of the wilderness so far we no longer remember that there is a border.

Civilization fears this wild Otherness and calls it wilderness, the place of the wild animal *(wild-deor)*. But what the human truly fears in the wild is loss of control, loss of power, and unsatisfied desire. All of these it must face in the wilderness, and so it seeks to eliminate it and turn the world into one human settlement, hoping that this will satisfy our longing and loneliness and fear.

This is the paradox of civilization, which stands in much of its splendor and light as a parody of the contemplative life, and thus as a parody of the true end of humanity.

What begins in augury as a desire to see the holy becomes a place of walls that bar the holy, because in eliminating wilderness we inadvertently lose touch with our way, which must lie through our relationship with the wild. This is nothing more (or less) than the originating energy that runs through all things: the force that gives form. "Self organizing, self-informing," as Gary Snyder defines it, this way of "Great Nature" is "not far from the Buddhist term *dharma* with its original senses of forming and firming."[4]

Our way is *this* way, discovered not by annihilating the wild but by *being* it.

It is in the tension between these two ideas that western civilization continues to play out its hand. Do we insist on melting them (whoever they are) into us in the hopes that their Otherness will vanish? Do we push the barbarian from our borders in the fantasy that we know who we are as long as they stay out there?

What do we do with the wild truth?

Templum is where we consider most deeply the stars; where we stand face to face with our own remote desire *(de-sidus:* from the star). It is ourselves we cut open in contemplation, precisely because it is the one place where we do not seek to satisfy our longing with false idols and addictions. In contemplation we lay ourselves open. In doing so we too become augurs, seers, visionaries, not because we have access to the sky but because we see in the sky a mirror for our own condition.

And yet almost everything in our culture teaches us to defend ourselves against this endless vulnerability.

One of Gerald May's patients describes this feeling; in his case it was the ending of an addiction. "Where alcohol had been," he said, "there was emptiness."

Gerald May then adds: "He described feeling scared of that emptiness when he would think about it, but he just let it be. Sometimes, when he normally would have been drinking, he just sat and looked at the sky. He did not feel pride about having quit drinking but he did feel good. His imprisonment was over."[5]

Looking at the sky he finds there—and not in the bottle—the hole that matches the hole in his heart. He knows that he is empty and finds a companion in the emptiness of the sky. He's entered the sanctuary, walked off the edge of the script, and instead has settled into open space. He's camping out under the stars, his life turning into a kind of poem. He is face to face with desire, which might be another name for the backside of God.

As May says, such a moment is not a matter of pride; it is a matter of humility, of humus. Maybe even humor. For once his feet are solidly on the ground. He looks to the sky not to escape but in simple recognition: home is now inside this vastness.

And so: "his imprisonment was over." Here we see freedom as the end of an addiction, or the facing of what the addiction means. The addiction is an attempt to fill the hole our desire creates. And yet desire is nothing but a road. It's the channel the river digs as it seeks its way to the sea. It's a natural force, a kind of gravity, the grief and weight that loving brings.

Rightly disciplined, desire binds us to this earth. What else is marriage but an ecstatic grounding of desire for the purpose of mutual transformation? Desire is the wild card hidden inside all sacrament.

Mountains and rivers, marriages and children—they're all a dance between ourselves and our wildest desire. They're paths that lead into that forest where all paths end.

This is now wilderness re-visioned, the way Dante finds the forest at the end of the *Purgatorio*. No longer the *selva oscura* in which he had once lost himself, it is now the *selva antica*, the ancient forest of an earthly paradise. Harrison calls this a "denatured forest," but I think that this misses something. It's not that the wilderness has been conquered; instead, the wilderness has *been faced.*

How does Jesus "defeat" Satan in the desert? How do the Israelites survive their forty years of wandering? Or St. Anthony, or the poet/hermit Han Shan? They win by surrendering themselves to the condition in which they find themselves. They do not succumb to whatever temptations arise, to "sin," which always has something to do with the desire to control the human condition—that is, in gaining sexual power, economic power, military power. Instead they remain steadfast and open, all windows and unbarred doors. They see the true shape of desire and stop seeking substitutes. They know it is the infinite in themselves they fear and long for in the Other. They sit and look at the sky.

The result? They become what they desire. Instead of alienation, relationship. For them the lion lies down with the lamb. The wilderness springs up a garden.

It's the face of a mountain or the sea; of a woman, as Dante writes, who makes us feel again the flames of that ancient desire. It's the sound of the wind, the waves, or of the radio tuned to the open road. Like a river it carries us away from ourselves.

2

Sometimes at the ocean I recall Robert Frost's wonderfully sardonic and sad poem describing the poor souls who spend their days at the beach just staring out to sea:

> The people along the sand
> All turn and look one way.
> They turn their back on the land.
> They look at the sea all day.
>
> As long as it takes to pass
> A ship keeps raising its hull;
> The wetter ground like glass
> Reflects a standing gull.
>
> The land may vary more;
> But wherever the truth may be—
> The water comes ashore,
> And the people look at the sea.
>
> They cannot look out far.
> They cannot look in deep.
> But when was that ever a bar
> To any watch they keep?[6]

Here, Frost implies, there is no relief from separateness. His onlookers are failed contemplatives who can neither embrace the complex and varying life on land nor reach any of the depths that appear to lie out at sea. Frost himself seems to suggest that such gazing is doomed to failure, but I think we are granted glimpses of what lies down under.

Indeed, I believe we hit the bottom of beauty when we discover there is no bottom. No longer is there a goal; we can cease our endless striving. Accustomed as we are to definition, this astonishingly open-ended love may terrify us.

"But as the mind . . . approaches more nearly to contemplation," writes Gregory of Nyssa, "it sees more clearly what of the divine nature is uncontemplated. . . . This is the seeing that consists in not seeing, because that which is sought transcends all knowledge, being separated on all sides by incomprehensibility as by a kind of darkness."

Gregory writes in the 4th century after Christ. He speaks of Moses' request from the wilderness of Mount Sinai to see God face to face: "He shone with glory. And although lifted up through such lofty experiences, he is still unsatisfied in his desire for more. He still thirsts for that with which he constantly filled himself to capacity. . . ."[7]

The temples we build by day we must destroy by night. The self we struggle to define as we mature we must later learn to undefine—through the wilderness of mountain, sea, desert; of prayer, art, love—so that the missing One will have a space to enter. And in that space the angel comes to us with his sword: we find ourselves cut open, our hearts and tongues replaced. We find ourselves beside ourselves.

"Such an experience seems to me to belong to the soul which loves what is beautiful," concludes Gregory. "Hope always draws the soul from the beauty which is seen to what is beyond, always kindles the desire for the hidden through what is constantly perceived. Therefore, the ardent lover of beauty, although receiving what is always visible as an image of what he desires, yet longs to be filled with the very stamp of the archetype."

"When poets," writes Paul Valery, "repair to the enchanted forest of language it is with the express purpose of getting lost. . . ."

We want to understand. We want clear boundaries and definitions. We want an end. And yet where is the end of *Lear*, of *The Magic Flute*? Where is the end of a mountain, that blue expanse of sky?

Gregory of Nyssa: "We can conceive then of no limitation in an infinite nature: and that which is limitless cannot by its nature be understood. And so every desire for the Beautiful, which draws us on in this ascent, is intensified by the soul's very progress towards it. And this is the real meaning of seeing God: never to have this desire satisfied."[8]

At our best we know what those heroic ones know, those described by a friend of Stephen Levine, who "dive right into love . . . they're never too old or too far gone to miss it. Moths to a flame. They know light. The more darkness surrounds them, the quicker they move toward it."⁹

Love, they know, is not in the explanations we give (which are mostly justifications). Love is in the creation of a space where the other is allowed the freedom to love in return. Where, indeed, the other is allowed to return, to turn again, like the prodigal we all are. Love cuts open the space that makes this possible. All of creation is intended as consecrated space, finite and without end. It is all bottomless bottom. And in this absence of an ending, in the poetry of the world, we dwell.

The word is only the edge of an infinite well. The image has a clarity all its own, but it is a clarity that is finally fathomless, the way any truth is. Where is the edge to any of us? At our very bottom is an absolute abyss of love, unending, awe-ful. This passion for God rages uncontrollably within us, wild and untamed and singing.

Conclusion

NOTES

1 See David Steindl-Rast, *Gratefulness* (New York: Paulist Press, 1984), p.62.

2 Harrison, *Forests: The Shadow of Civilization* (Chicago: University of Chicago Press), p.6.

3 See, along with Harrison, Dolores LaChapelle, *Sacred Land, Sacred Sex: Rapture of the Deep* (Silverton Cob: Fine Hill Arts, 1988) p. 210. "The human longing to experience again the slanting rays of the sun through the high curved ribs of the tree was the inspiration of Gothic cathedrals." She quotes a specialist on medieval architecture, who claims that "the Gothic arch is the shape of two upright saplings tied together at the top as in a neolithic hut. The cathedral congregation, facing the east window, is a reenactment of a Teutonic tribe facing the barbaric sun-god Balder through the door of the hut."

4 Gary Snyder, *Practice of the Wild* (San Francisco: North Point Press, 1990), p.10.

5 Gerald May, *Addiction and Grace* (San Francisco: Harper and Row, 1988), p.157.

6 Robert Frost, "Neither Out Far Nor in Deep," in his *Collected Poems* (New York: Holt, Rinehart and Winston, 1969).

7 Gregory of Nyssa, from *Life of Moses* II, excerpted in *Light From Light: An Anthology of Christian Mysticism,* edited by Louis Dupre and James A. Wiseman (New York: Paulist Press, 1988) pp. 55–57.

8 Stephen Levine, *Who Dies* (New York: Anchor Books, 1982), p. 178.

9 Gregory of Nyssa, *Life of Moses* II. See Andrew Louth, *The Origins of the Christian Mystical Tradition* (Clarendon: Oxford University Press, 1981), p 88.

Biographical Note

Doug Thorpe is the author of *A New Earth*, *A Study of the Pearl*, *George Herbert's Temple* and *William Blake's Jerusalem*, and is the editor of the anthology *Work and the Life of the Spirit*. His essays have appeared in *Parabola*, *Terra Nova*, *Image*, *Mars Hill Review*, *The Christian Century* and other journals. He teaches literature and writing at Seattle Pacific University, provides poetry for Earth Ministry's *Earth Letter*, which he used to edit, and provides spiritual direction for students and others in the Seattle area. He is married with one child, who has momentarily forsaken the Northwest mountains for the east coast.